The Day
Human King

The Day Human Trilogy

Book 2

B. Kristin McMichael

Lexia Press, LLC
P.O. Box 982
Worthington, OH 43085
www.lexiapress.com

ISBN-10: 1941745970
ISBN-13: 978-1-941745-97-7

Cover design: Ravven, http://www.ravven.com
Editor: Kathie Middlemiss of Kat's Eye Editing
Melissa of There For You Editing
Proofing: Ashton M. Brammer

CONTENTS

CHAPTER 1

Devin Alexander was already sick of the sidhe. All they did was complain, including his bonded night human, Vanessa McKinny. Thankfully, she had fallen asleep in his arms, and he could enjoy a bit of silence. It wasn't that he expected much more from her; she was now responsible for dealing with all of the sidhe, and he couldn't help her much because they were terrified of him. After he'd taken away their magic at the end of her sham of a trial, most of them steered clear of him or ran away at the sight of him. He could walk anywhere around the palace and not have to deal with a single sidhe. Unfortunately, it wasn't the same for Nessa. They constantly called on her for decisions about one thing or another. From the moment they'd taken over the sidhe, there'd been endless complaining. Nessa turned to Devin with her frustrations since he was the only one she could complain to. He understood … but the silence was nice. He could finally retreat to his own thoughts.

Devin was a day human stuck in the night human world. He'd spent his childhood surrounded by night humans who sucked blood to live, but never once had he been the one that others feared. He'd had no special powers, and everyone had always been more powerful than him. Until Lord Randolph had begun training him, Devin was the one who lived in fear. One particular night human had killed his entire family, leaving him paralyzed at the sight of night humans until he learned how to defend himself. It wasn't a good memory, but one he would never change. He hadn't known then what the dangerous night human world was, but now he was immersed in it. He didn't regret his life, however. The night human world brought him Nessa.

Finally, Nessa was peacefully asleep. She didn't want to turn people away—they came to her seeking assistance with planning and a need for help—but Devin did. They had spent the last few days running from assassins and fighting for their lives, and had almost died on several occasions. However, everyone had forgotten all about that, and wanted a piece of their time when they needed to rest. It was only hours ago that Devin was fatally stabbed, but that didn't seem to matter to the sidhe. When dawn broke, the sidhe should have headed off to bed, but didn't. So Devin thanked the people who were waiting and told them to come back another time before he whisked Nessa away. Luckily, their fear made them not refuse his request.

Once they were back in her room, Nessa instantly fell asleep. They both were so exhausted that they didn't even have time to talk about the day. Unfortunately, the next day wouldn't be any easier since they needed to get ready for the coronation. In fact, in less than seventy-two hours Nessa would be queen, and technically—since Devin was bonded to her—he would be king.

Devin gently slipped his arm out from under her head. Even though he was exhausted, he was feeling the side effects of all the power he had received. For some reason, the former sidhe king, Nessa's grandfather, had felt it necessary to give Devin his immense sidhe powers. Devin was unsure how the old man had done it, but he could now feel the sidhe magic running through his veins and sleep wasn't coming to him. Combined with the fact he rarely slept more than four hours in a normal day anyway, Devin was on a bit of a power high. There was no way he was falling asleep any time soon.

Nessa's eyes cracked open as he laid her head on her pillow. He had hoped she would stay asleep throughout the night.

Devin leaned down close to her. "I'll be back soon," he said quietly. "I'm just going for a run to burn off my extra energy."

Nessa sleepily nodded and tugged at the front of his shirt. When he leaned in closer and softly kissed her, she mumbled something against his lips, and then let go of him. Devin took in a deep breath of her flowery scent and stood back up, unable to believe that she was his. His world had been turned upside down the moment she saved his life by bonding to him, and had gotten even more confusing when he realized he wanted to be bonded to her. He wasn't looking to fall in love again, but somehow she'd found a way into his heart. She was still Nessa, and that would never change, but something in him transformed. She was now *his* Nessa.

Devin stopped at the doorway and looked at the invisible assassins standing guard. The four women that had guarded the old sidhe king were now standing watch for Nessa. Since they were needed and Nessa had to be protected, he hadn't taken the magic to hide oneself away from them. He nodded to the unseen women and went on his way down the hall.

Closing his eyes, he used his sidhe magic and searched the whole palace. With his new powers, he could feel each and every sidhe if he tried. He didn't want to run into anyone else. Their fear alone was laughable, but all of the bowing and running in terror wore on him after the first five minutes. He quickly found the clearest route through the palace and took off running. He needed to burn this energy if he planned to sleep anytime in the next week.

Devin listened to the sound of his shoes hitting the pounded-down earth at his feet as he lost himself within his own thoughts, running alongside the ornately woven trees that made up the walls. He had only arrived at the sidhe village days ago, and now he had to stay. His whole life had been turned upside-down in such a short time. First, he was bound to Nessa. He wasn't minding that too much now, but their original goal had been to break the bond. However, upon meeting the sidhe king, everything had changed. Devin now had a role and responsibility to the sidhe people. Yes, he had been planning to search for a purpose in life after unbinding from Nessa, but he never thought one would fall into his lap like this. His purpose was thrust upon him in the form of sidhe magical powers. Devin had much to learn about the gift he was given to keep Nessa safe and change the sidhe, yet he didn't know how long he had to figure everything out. Her coronation was in less than three days, and he was sure the other five families wouldn't sit by nicely and let her claim the throne without a fight.

The sidhe clans were divided into five families, and everyone owed loyalty to one of them. When Nessa's grandfather took over permanently, the others had no choice. The old man was powerful, and no one could tell him *no*. When Nessa assumed power in three days, Devin wouldn't be nearly as powerful as the old man because he didn't know how to use the power he was given. In fact, he knew very little about the sidhe in general. The late king told him his power was to do anything the sidhe could do, but Devin didn't know what they *could* do. Nessa's rise to the throne wouldn't be as easy as her grandfather's was.

Devin turned down a hallway that was lined with open windows. When he saw the walls around the palace, he considered trying to leave out of any of the various vine-laced doors. Nessa wasn't allowed to leave without the palace knowing, but was that the case for Devin? Would the alarms sound? He did have a bit of Nessa's blood within him, but he wasn't the future sovereign. Was he free to come and go as he pleased? Could he leave the village if he wanted? Something told him he could not. Taking the power from the previous king to protect Nessa came with the bond of being stuck to the sidhe for the rest of his life. The thought was both terrifying and reassuring. Without intending to, Devin had found his place in the world.

He watched the sun shine through the windows and changed his course. It was too tempting to see outside and not be able to go as he pleased. He needed a more interior route for his run in order to avoid the temptation of walking out of the doorway.

Devin began running down another cleared hallway. He liked that the sidhe avoided him, but he couldn't dodge them forever; he was going to have to deal with them eventually. He wasn't quite sure where to begin, but hopefully he would after learning more about them and the powers he now had.

Coming to a turn again, he stopped suddenly at the person in front of him. He had put a spell on the palace to not allow anyone to use magic to cover themselves unless he allowed it, like the sidhe assassins protecting Nessa. Before, he had been the only one to see through the magic, but now everyone saw exactly who everyone else was. It was Devin's first step in stopping all of the deception. His sudden halt was because of the sidhe standing in his way: Fiona Ferguson. She was the daughter and only child left of the Ferguson family, one of the five that traditionally held power. Fiona had been rumored to have been Nessa's older brother's lover before he ran off two months ago to attempt to win over Arianna Grace, a more powerful night human, and Devin's former charge.

Fiona stared in shock at Devin, her mouth in an obvious '*oh*.' She hadn't been expecting to see him, either, and the powerful, cunning sidhe wasn't as prepared as she normally was to play the power game.

Devin had been wondering about one aspect the day before. When Nessa led him to her grandfather, they had passed through a crypt that was only open to someone of the McKinny line. Suddenly, Devin realized how Finn, Fiona's brother, had followed them through the McKinny family crypt. Because it was the last piece of the puzzle he couldn't figure out, Devin had been thinking it over since they left the crypt. How did Finn trick the wards on the crypt to get through? Only blood family could open the door, and Devin was sure they hadn't left it open.

"Day Human Prince," Fiona said quietly, bowing her head to him. She didn't run in fear, but her heartbeat had picked up. He was sure now that he was never meant to see the secret she carried. Coronation wasn't going to go as easy as Devin hoped.

Fiona Ferguson was pregnant with the former king's child.

Devin stood in the hallway and watched Fiona as she hurried away. She had to be at least seven months along, if not more. He scratched his head, wondering how he'd missed that disguise the past few days. He could see through their spells, but he hadn't seen that one coming. He was hoping with the fear that they all had of him that it would be easy to get Nessa on the throne with no complications. They had less than three days to the coronation … and the pregnancy of Fiona Ferguson was a complication.

He began his run again, but instead of staying inside, he turned into the open courtyard surrounding the palace. What he really needed was to escape the palace, and the sidhe world in general, but he couldn't just run away. Going for a run through the village would have to do for now.

Devin went around the open doorways that dotted the

fence around the palace. He wasn't sure if he could just leave without setting off alarms, but Nessa had shown him one gate out that her brother had charmed to let royalty through. Rhys apparently wasn't fond of the restrictions, either. Devin found the gate and kept running into the city that surrounded the palace. These were his people now, and this was his home, even though he knew nothing about the place.

Dawn was breaking, and most of the people were shutting up their homes before heading to bed. Almost all of the night humans were sensitive to some form of sunlight; whether it be that they couldn't be touched by any at all, or simply needed to avoid the strongest sunlight during the middle of the day. Even though Devin was used to the night human world and the opposite life they led, he still needed sunshine; he would always be a day human.

Devin slowed his run to look at the buildings he passed. The sidhe world mystified him. It was intricately designed, and had many hidden aspects that fascinated him. It may have been because he was an outsider, but he was awed by the work that made the forest into a city. Trees were grown and woven together to create homes that were as functional as those Devin was raised in, but everything about them were living. He could make out the slight opening that had to be a gate to a property. He was also getting better at seeing the sidhe. They integrated so well with nature that it was easy for normal day humans to pass by them without seeing them. The longer he was in their world, the more he saw.

As he ran further down the path, the homes were right next to each other with very little space between. He passed home after home, and no one was outside. As the road split in two, Devin took the left pathway, vowing to come back another day and go right. The common sidhe world fascinated him, unlike the elite sidhe he had been confined to since he had arrived here.

These were his people now. He wasn't born one of them, nor was he raised one of them, but they were his now, and they needed him. Nessa was enough reason to stay in the village, but her grandfather had made it a permanent decision by giving Devin sidhe powers. The old man's last dying wish was for Devin to save the sidhe. Devin had no clue how or what the old man meant. He was just a day human who knew nothing about the sidhe. This was his first venture outside of the palace alone, and there wasn't a sidhe in sight. They were still a mystery to him. One he needed to unravel.

The road bent again, and Devin turned the corner, coming face-to-face with the first sidhe that didn't know who he was … an old man trudged along the path, pulling a cart. Devin slowed beside him.

"Do you need help?" Devin offered. *The best way to get to know the sidhe*, he decided, *was to talk to them*. Devin was afraid they would view him as an outsider as a day human, but he had to try. He needed to learn more.

The old man was startled by him, and dropped one of the sides of the cart he was holding as he pulled. Luckily, Devin reached forward and caught the cart before it tipped sideways. It was stacked with canisters that seemed to be full for the most part. The old man eyed him over, but nodded when Devin took both sides of the cart to pull it. The old man hobbled alongside him.

"Yer not from around here," the old man finally said after they had walked a bit. He was covered in dust and dirt, and walked with a limp. There was a slight accent when he talked. The man was old and had to be full of knowledge, and it appeared he would be a good person to befriend.

"No," Devin replied. The cart wasn't heavy, but he didn't understand why the man was pulling it; he wasn't in any shape to be walking a long distance, let alone with a cart in tow.

The man grunted and gave a brief nod. It was obvious to all night humans that Devin was a day human. Even with sidhe power, Devin still had day human blood, which he was sure the man could smell. Fortunately, this left Devin in a place of not being a sidhe, and allowed to ask obvious questions without ridicule.

"Why do you—" Devin began to ask, but the man smiled and finished his sentence.

"Take the cart around?" the man added. "Because we need to be fed, and this is my job. Around here we all do our part, and I can't just take the day off because my mare needs rest. People depend on me, and I depend on others. It's the way the world is supposed to work."

They walked further down the path, and a doorway opened to one of the hidden houses when they approached. Devin noticed the outline only after it was unfastened. He was going to have to look closer to actually be able to see where all of the sidhe lived. It was confusing, yet beautiful.

"Mary and Marybeth," the man greeted the woman and smaller child that stood there watching Devin curiously. The old man hobbled to them to retrieve the pitcher in the woman's hands.

Devin stood at the cart and watched as the old man returned to fill the pitcher from one of the full bottles in his cart. White liquid dripped from his ladle as he scooped several times to fill the pitcher. Placing the cap back on the container, the old man limped back to the woman and gave her the now full jug. She smiled graciously at the old man.

"Thank you. New assistant?" the one named Mary asked, still looking Devin over. He was out of place in the village, but it was a good feeling to be out of place and questioned rather than feared and avoided.

"Nah, just a young lad with manners. They don't raise them like that anymore," the man replied with a chuckle.

The lady nodded and pulled the little girl inside the house. That was enough of an explanation for her. Devin could feel already that his place was amongst the common sidhe. They didn't fear him, and they didn't pry. They were fine with him just being a day human and someone that wanted to know more. The old man began walking again. Devin took the cart to follow beside him.

"You deliver milk?" Devin asked, incredulous that the liquid in the jars was milk and not blood.

The old man laughed so hard he had to stop walking. Devin didn't find his question funny. He had seriously thought the old man was delivering blood when he'd heard liquid sloshing around in the canisters. In the night human world, people lived on blood. Therefore if there was something that needed to be delivered, Devin assumed it would be blood, not milk. The old man wiped a few stray tears away.

"What sort of world do you come from, lad? That much blood? We are civilized people here," the old man replied. He smiled as he talked because he found Devin very amusing.

"I lived at a dearg-dul estate out west before coming here," Devin replied. They were quite civilized, too, and needed blood daily, like any night human.

The old man stopped laughing and nodded as they began their walk again. That was enough of an explanation for the man to understand. While the sidhe purposely kept themselves isolated from the rest of the night human world, they knew much about the other clans. The old man, no doubt, knew about the dearg-dul night humans that raised Devin.

"Not been here long, I take it," the man said, starting to hobble along the path again and leading the way.

"A couple of days," Devin replied, picking up the cart and

following alongside.

"Yet you have been around night humans before," the man added. Devin nodded. "Yes, milk. What did you think was in there?" the man asked, but his tone hinted that he knew the answer. He wasn't done teasing Devin yet.

Devin shrugged, a little embarrassed by his assumption. The old man halted, waiting for Devin to answer. The silence was uncomfortable. Suddenly, the man laughed again, throwing back his old, thinly haired head in the process. He was having an amusing time with Devin's assumptions.

"I bet you thought it was blood, right, day human?" the man guessed. "What did you think? We're savages that need a pitcher of blood a day? Isn't that a bit excessive?"

It wasn't in Devin's eyes. He had watched as Arianna—the girl he'd spent his life protecting until he met Nessa—consumed more than that a day after she changing into a night human. "That would be nothing compared to what the night humans that raised me used," Devin replied with a shrug. There was nothing to be embarrassed about since the old man had guessed his answer.

"*Raised* by night humans. As in you were treated as one of them?" the old man questioned. Devin nodded. He was more than one of them. He had been Lord Randolph's right-hand man for years. "That explains a lot. I did wonder why a day human would wander freely amongst us without fear."

It was true. Devin didn't fear night humans, nor did he fear the sidhe … even before he'd gotten his new power. The deargdul clan of vampire-like people that raised him could drink a pitcher of blood per person every day. They all preferred fresh blood from live day humans. Devin should have been scared being a day human and thus food, but he was not. He didn't fear them—as he was never the one they were looking to drink from—but they still needed a lot of blood to survive, especially right after they turned on their sixteenth birthday. Devin couldn't pinpoint when his fear went away, exactly, yet night humans were no longer scary as they were when he was a child.

The man looked Devin over again, like he was searching for a clue to tell him why Devin was the way he was. He wouldn't find it. Devin didn't even know why he was the way he was.

"Raised with the dearg-dul, and you're still standing? I thought they killed all of their victims." The man stopped at another hidden house. A woman similarly dressed as the other, in the greens and browns of the forest, was waiting for them. The man filled her pitcher before returning to the cart to continue talking.

"They do need quite a lot of blood, but they typically only kill on their changing night. Otherwise, they just use multiple donors per week to stay fed, or at least the elite do. The commoners feed once a week from supplies given to them," Devin replied. The dearg-dul were not as scary as everyone thought they were. They had saved him and raised him after his family was killed. They had a system, and it worked.

"So you were the elite?" The man had made the assumption from Devin's comment. He was perceptive for his old age and run-down body.

"Kind of," Devin replied. He wasn't big on talking about himself.

The old man got the hint and didn't ask any more personal questions. Devin followed alongside him silently. They kept walking, stopping every now and then at specific doors to deliver the milk. The man would fill whatever jug they brought him with milk before moving on. Each person stared at Devin, but none were afraid. It made it easy to feel like he could fit into the sidhe world as long as he was outside of the palace. As the path began to have fewer houses along it, the old man was ready to talk again.

"Can I ask why you're here? We don't get too many day humans." The man was curious. That much Devin could answer.

"I was only planning a short visit, and now it seems I can't leave," Devin replied, not giving away too many details. If the old man knew who Devin really was, there was no possible way he would continue talking to him. Devin already knew what the elite sidhe thought of him, as they ran in fear. Devin had no clue about the common sidhe, therefore he was trying to avoid the same reaction.

When the old man paused at the end of the road, Devin could make out a hidden house. It was getting easier because he had a chance to study each house that opened their doors for the old man on their walk. Behind a fence, which looked more like hedges that happened to grow side-by-side, animals roamed in a clearing in the woods. It seemed like they were free to wander, but the fence was expertly crafted to blend right into the scenery. Devin pulled the cart to the house and let go of it.

"Your guide here forgot to tell you that no one is allowed out, I suppose," the man commented.

"No, she didn't mention that," Devin replied, shaking his head with a smile. Nessa had left out that detail, but that wasn't what was keeping him now. He'd have to ask her later about that rule. It seemed like she left out most of the rules when she brought him into her world.

"Oh, it was a girl." The man chuckled. "Always a girl."

Devin nodded in agreement. He couldn't deny that it was Nessa. She was the reason behind everything now. He was in the sidhe world because of Nessa, but more than that, he was alive because of her. She had saved his life … more than once.

The old man walked over and unlatched a hidden door through the hedge fence.

"How do you get your blood?" Devin asked the question that had been playing on his mind. If the old man was delivering milk, how much blood did a sidhe even need? Nessa told him they didn't need much, and their magic came from nature not blood. He had only once given her his own blood, and he had never seen her drink it otherwise.

The man smiled. "I wondered if you would ask. Once a year there's a festival. The elite bring in the blood for us, and we hold a feast. That's all of the blood we need to survive. Nothing like the world you come from."

"Once a year?" Devin inquired. That was a bit extreme for any night human, but it did explain the man's age. He had never seen an aged dearg-dul before, at least physically aged. No matter the night human species, blood kept them young. The man who had saved him as a child was already an old man by the time he'd found Devin, yet he never looked any older than the day he saved him.

"Yes, just once a year," the man replied like it made complete sense.

"And the sidhe don't need more blood than that?" Devin asked in disbelief. It was really an odd concept for him.

"Need?" the old man replied, and then shrugged. "We are only commoners here. Our needs are regulated by those that know better." He sounded a little bitter, but he kept his words formal.

Devin got the hint. One more thing the elite sidhe regulated in their village. Devin understood then that sidhe needed blood more than once a year, but they just weren't allowed to have it. The elite weren't gaining any points in Devin's opinion. He had yet to find any redeeming qualities in the men and women he was supposed to lead. Devin mentally noted the lack of blood as one more thing he needed to change. The dearg-dul lived on greater quantities of blood and they were fine. They didn't have to kill for it, and there was always more than enough to go around. Devin would have to change that for the common sidhe. There had to be a solution.

The man returned to Devin and took the cart up to the fence opening.

"Thank you, lad, for your help. I do the best I can, and the people around here depend on me," he explained. "If my mare would get better, it would be easier, but that isn't the problem. We all do our part to keep the village running. If you must stay, remember to find your place in this world. No matter day or night human, there is room for everyone here, and everyone can help each other."

Devin nodded and turned to walk away back the way they came. He was beginning to understand the common sidhe a bit more.

"I don't know where I can fit in with the elite," Devin replied before walking away. "They aren't quite to my liking."

"Let me change that advice, then." Devin paused and turned back. The old man's eyes hardened. "The first chance you get, run as far away from here as you can. The sidhe elite are horrible to day humans. There is room for a day human in the village, but there isn't in the palace. You would do better in the woods than under their roof."

Devin nodded his head and walked back down the path. He would run away if he could. Even if he could leave Nessa behind, he was stuck in the sidhe village. Devin had considered kidnapping Nessa and whisking her away, but that wouldn't work, either. The sidhe needed Nessa with her different views. Before Devin implemented his new rules on assassins, the elite were slowly killing each other off. The sidhe needed change, and Devin was the one who had to figure out how, not just for his own sake, but for Nessa's.

The old man's opinion would change suddenly when he

found out that Devin was living in the palace. Devin would be sure to keep it a secret as to whom he really was. The commoner sidhe didn't seem to like the elite as much as the elite liked to pretend they did. Devin could see where he needed to start with change, and it wasn't the commoners. Now he just needed to make a plan to do so.

Devin meandered back down the pathway he had come from. Every now and then, he paused at the houses he remembered giving milk to as they'd passed. He was trying to see more and understand the sidhe. It was hard to make out the outlines of most of the doorways. The world was hidden, even in their normal environment. Devin was unsure how you would even change people who hide from each other. As he passed the first doorway he had stopped at with the old man, the door cracked open. The little girl from before appeared, staring up at him.

"Day human," she said shyly in her little girl voice. She couldn't have been more than five or six years old. "Mommy said to make sure and give you this on your way." The little girl stayed in the doorway, watching Devin, holding out a cloth with something wrapped inside it. She didn't fear him, but she also was very tentative.

Devin slowly walked over to the girl. She was analyzing him. Devin realized that it wasn't fear that made her hesitant; she was just taking in every detail about him. He was probably one of the first day humans she had ever met. Devin took the cloth and unwrapped it. Unexpectedly, two warm buns were carefully waiting for him.

"Momma wanted to thank you for helping Old Man Winters," the girl said as she sat down on the stoop.

Feeling that the girl wanted to talk more, Devin sat next to the child. She didn't shy away from him, and continued to take in every detail.

"You dress funny," the girl said, looking closer at his clothing, especially his jeans. Devin wasn't dressed the same as the sidhe, and it didn't bother him. He wasn't one of them—at least not completely.

"Ah, but to me you dress funny," Devin replied, taking a bite of one bun. It was sweet and hot from the oven. He hadn't been that hungry, but now found it was a nice morning treat to have.

The little girl laughed. "I'm not funny. Everyone dresses like this." The girl patted her light green dress proudly. All of the sidhe did dress like her, and in her world that must have been everyone.

Devin smiled with his full mouth. Her laughter was great to hear. In fact, he couldn't think of any other laughter he had heard since he'd come into the village. It was refreshing to be away from the palace. The commoner sidhe were much more normal in Devin's eyes. There wasn't the evil behind them. They were continuing on and making daily life work for them.

Devin looked at the girl as he ate. He saw nothing about her that even made him think of a night human. She was as close to a normal day human as any day human he had met. It could simply be that she hadn't changed into a night human yet, or it could be that they weren't different from day humans in their normal form. Devin had to wonder when they transformed into night humans. In other clans, some were at birth, and others later in life. He tried to find an image of a commoner sidhe that reminded him of a night human, but he could think of no one he had passed on his walk thus far that was a scary night human.

"I've never seen a day human before," the little girl told him.

"I'd guess not," Devin replied after he swallowed what he was chewing on. "I haven't seen any since I've been here, either." That was true. The sidhe village seemed devoid of any human not sidhe.

"Why are you here?" the girl asked. It was obvious that Devin was a new source of wonder for the young girl, and therefore she was full of questions.

Devin shrugged and took another bite. *Why was he there?* There were over a dozen answers, but they were all too complicated to give as an answer to a child.

"Do they treat you well?" she asked before he could come up with an answer for the last question.

Devin smiled. Her interest amused him. Most of the sidhe just passed by and never gave him a second thought in the village. This child wanted to know more than anyone else had asked. Devin saw the promise in the younger sidhe; they were worth saving if he could figure it out.

"I'm doing fine. It isn't like my home, but I can adjust," Devin replied. She sounded like she was trying to be adult, and so he gave her a grown-up answer.

"You're from the outside?" the girl asked, her eyes twinkling at the thought.

"Yes, but now I'm from here," Devin answered.

"As in you're staying?" she asked, disappointed. Maybe she was already dreaming about the adventure Devin could take her on outside of the sidhe walls. Smiling, he shook his head. Thousands of thoughts were passing through her young mind. He had forgotten what children were like.

"Yes. The girl I love is here, so I'll be staying," he explained, sorry to disappoint her.

"A sidhe?" the girl asked in a whisper. She'd latched on to what he'd said like it was a big secret.

"Yes, she is," Devin replied, also in a whisper, though he had no idea why.

"You need to be careful," the girl added in hushed tones.

"They don't allow sidhe and day humans to fall in love."

Devin had to grin at her response, and quickly tried to hide his reaction. He didn't choose to fall in love with Nessa ... it just kind of happened. To have a young child tell him about love was a bit amusing.

"They don't even allow people from different sidhe families to marry," the girl continued, not noticing his quick smile. "You'll end up with my older brother in the castoff camp. He's been there three years since he married the wrong family. Now we can't even see him."

"Castoffs?" Devin questioned. He as pretty sure they weren't on an island.

"That's where they force people to live if they break the rules, like falling in love with the wrong person," she explained. She was quite young, yet very sure of the rules.

Devin had begun to think the common sidhe were fine and actually lived in harmony until he had heard that. She didn't seem to support, or understand, the silly rule, but it was already ingrained in her, and that was a scary thought. She was too young to have to think, or worry, about falling in love. He'd believed the commoners were better, but maybe not. He couldn't imagine forcing people apart for something such as love.

"Who sends them there?" Devin asked. He wasn't even sure how the commoner sidhe community was set up, government wise. It was all too new to him. Did they have a council, like the elite?

"The elite elders," the girl whispered again.

Devin nodded. *No.* The common sidhe were living a good life, but the elite were the ones messing everything up. Why did it even matter to the elite who a commoner married? It seemed silly and petty, like they were just doing things to assert their power. Devin had no clue how he was going to change the sidhe, but he knew it would have to be start with the elite. They were set on their ruling, and didn't seem to care who it hurt. The change had to come from within the palace for the good of all the sidhe.

"Marybeth," her mother called from within the house.

The little girl stood, causing her curls to bounce, and smiled at Devin.

"Where do the castoffs live?" Devin asked. He needed to see for himself ... needed to see all of the sidhe to figure out what had to be done to help them.

"If you take a left at the ever-flowering tree back that way, it ends at a dirt path. It isn't like the rest of the roads. Back there," the girl explained, pointing down the road Devin had come from before she opened the door to her house wide enough to slip in.

"Tell your mother thank you," Devin said as the girl smiled at him. "They were delicious."

Devin stood and began walking back toward the palace. He had spent all day outside, wandering while the sidhe slept, and now he noticed the day was ending. The sun was lowering on the horizon, which meant Nessa would surely be waking soon. He needed to head back to her side. He didn't want her to worry, at least not too much. He would have to see the rest of the village, and the castoff camp, later.

CHAPTER 2

Nessa **woke from** her sleep to find the space beside her cold. Devin was gone, and had been for a while. She vaguely remembered him leaving, but she'd also assumed he would come back soon. He was just going for a run, which shouldn't take all day. She used the bond between them to track him down, and found him wandering around the village outside of the palace walls. She should have known that by showing him the one gate to leave he wouldn't stay in the palace. It didn't matter, though; she was certain he wasn't going to leave her. She already knew that much because the bond told her. He was dedicated to staying beside her.

Moving to the bathroom, Nessa dressed quickly while her thoughts still wandered. Now she could easily enter his mind at any time, though she tried not to. She hadn't given it much thought after they were initially bonded, and she'd made sure to stay out of his mind in the hopes that he would stay out of hers. It was weird to be intimately connected with another person. Even worse was that she couldn't control her emotions as well as he could, and she was sure he could feel what she felt, some of which was very embarrassing. She'd never had feelings for someone like she did for Devin. It was new and exciting, yet very terrifying.

She was still shocked that he was hers forever. Things had

changed in minutes after her grandfather had awoken and saved them. Nessa loved Devin—of that she was sure—almost as much as she hated him at times. It wasn't exactly like what she'd thought love would be, but something about Devin had always felt right. He had a past, had loved another deeply, but she could see in his mind that she was the only one for him now. He was devoted to her, and she didn't know how to act around that.

A knock at the door brought her attention back to reality. Nessa stood and walked over to it. It was a good thing she had already dressed. The sidhe didn't seem to ever stop. She was surprised everyone had stayed away long enough for her to sleep. Since coming into power of the sidhe, it seemed something was always needed from her. She would have to grow used to it since the coronation was only days away, but it was still different. Nessa was extremely thankful Devin would be beside her, as she was sure he was the only reason she'd gotten any sleep at all. They all feared him. She cracked the door, discovering that her uncle stood on the other side. She smiled at him and opened the door widely to invite him in.

"I grabbed a tray for you on my way, figuring you wouldn't have eaten yet. Breakfast?" he asked, holding a platter for her.

Nodding, Nessa took it from him as he walked into the front part of her apartment. Devin had released the blood spell they had placed on her apartment a little to allow people to visit her in private, but Nessa knew why. She could see the four assassins in the room with her. Devin had left her protection.

'And you couldn't at least take one with you?' Nessa asked Devin across the bond. Four assassins as protection was a bit much.

Devin laughed. *'Good morning, princess.'*

Nessa huffed and her uncle looked up to her with worried eyes. Since she had returned from the crypt after seeing her grandfather, his father, he was a bit sensitive around her. Nessa shook her head, trying to get him to not worry.

'Come on, Nessa,' Devin added. 'Who's going to mess with me now? Everyone is afraid of me.' That much was true. Her uncle was sitting here, his eyes growing wide in fear that he had upset her or Devin.

"Just talking to Devin." She pointed to her head as she explained to ease her uncle's anxiety.

'You could have been a bit nicer, and maybe they wouldn't fear you,' Nessa replied. It truly was Devin's own doing that he'd scared the crap out of the elite sidhe. Nessa secretly thought that he was happy they feared him because they left him alone.

'I doubt that. The first view of your grandfather's swords would have told them enough,' Devin replied. He was making his way back to her.

It didn't matter if Devin was in the room or not, all of the sidhe in the palace—beyond Ronan and Gemma—feared him, and thus feared upsetting Nessa and bringing down Devin's wrath. It had been slightly comedic for the first ten minutes, but now Nessa was getting annoyed with it. Everyone was careful with what they said and how they said it. Devin's new powers made everyone afraid of his wrath, including Uncle Rolf. Hoping that Devin wasn't present, Uncle Rolf relaxed and sat down with her.

"He's not with you?" Rolf asked, trying to look casually around the room and reassure himself that he was safe. He was still a little strung out being alone in her room since he wasn't that comfortable with the new Devin yet.

"No, he is out in the village, going for a walk," she replied, taking a bite of the food her uncle had brought.

"In the village?" Rolf repeated what she had just said, his voice a mixture of confusion and disgust.

Nessa nodded. The elite sidhe never went into the village

for just a stroll. They only went out when going from family compound to family compound. Elite sidhe saw no use for the common sidhe beyond ruling them. She was raised to think she was better than the common sidhe, just as all of the elite had been raised, but the lessons never really stuck well with Nessa. She had seen plenty to wonder who the people were. She'd asked her teachers enough questions about the differences—which didn't really exist—that they stopped answering. Nessa knew then that there was no real difference, just prejudice. Devin's new fascination with the common sidhe didn't bother her at all.

"Why would he do that?" Rolf asked, completely perplexed.

"Probably to learn more. He knows very little about the sidhe," Nessa replied, taking a second bite.

"What could he learn from them? If he wants to be taught, we can arrange for someone in the palace to tutor him," Rolf suggested. Nessa hid her smile with her napkin. No one in the palace would be willing to be alone with Devin; she knew that much. Nessa shrugged. There was no use explaining to her uncle that maybe the common sidhe were the best ones to teach Devin. They didn't fear him yet.

The food tasted off—there must have been a new cook—so she set it down, unable bring herself to finish it. She'd have to go down to the kitchen and find her own food later. She had time since Devin was still out, even though he was slowly making his way back.

"What brings you by, Uncle?" Nessa asked. She knew he wasn't there just to deliver her food.

"It's customary for the new ruler to sit and listen to grievances before you ascend the throne. That leaves us two days to get through the whole list of people who wish to plead their case before you." Uncle Rolf pulled out a list and handed it to Nessa. "There seems to be an increase from when your brother ascended. I'm guessing everyone figures since you're a girl they might have a better chance."

She took the list and paged through it. It was three pages of columns of names. Two days didn't seem like much time if she had to listen to hundreds of people plead their cases. How long did each case take? How many people would she have to listen to at one time? Would they each tell their side, or was it just a one-sided complaint? Nessa had no clue what it really meant to decide on grievances. She should have paid more attention to her tutors when she was growing up. There was very little about the whole process of becoming the queen that she knew about, and suddenly Nessa felt a bit light-headed. The whole thing was overwhelming. Everything since she had returned was happening too fast.

"What exactly do I have to do?" Nessa asked, setting the list down on the seat next to her. Now she felt a bit sick.

"They come before you one at a time to tell you their problem and how they'd like it solved. You just either approve or deny their request. It isn't much," Rolf explained. He didn't seem to find the list overwhelming. In fact, he actually made it sound quite simple.

Nessa felt queasy, and her legs had begun tingling, too. She contemplated standing and rushing off to the bathroom. She felt off, but not quite that off yet. However, that was quickly changing. Maybe she was worse than she thought. She wasn't sure she would make it to the bathroom if she did need to puke. Whatever she ate really hadn't agreed with her.

'What's wrong?' Devin asked. He knew the moment she'd taken ill. Their bond had grown stronger as the days passed. She felt his worry, too.

'I don't know,' Nessa replied, and she truly didn't. One moment she was fine, and the next she was ill. *'I feel sick.'* That was the only way she could describe it. It wasn't like she had

much to compare to it. The sidhe rarely got sick and she could even remember the last time clearly, but that was the only answer she could give him.

'What kind of sick?' Devin demanded as he broke out in a full sprint back to the palace. He took her feelings more serious than she did.

'I think I ate something that was bad,' Nessa replied, trying to calm his now fast-beating heart. She could feel the anxiety pour off him. It was just a bad cook. How could she explain that to him? She doubted he would stop to listen now.

'Don't go anywhere. I'll be back to you in two minutes,' Devin ordered her. The female assassins in the room moved closer, as if Devin had talked to them, also.

'I'm fine,' she tried to reassure him as she closed her eyes. Her head had begun to pound. Maybe it was the never getting sick thing that made it worse when she finally did fall ill. Being a sidhe wasn't all that great if that was the case.

"Vanessa?" Rolf asked. He was kneeling before her now. She didn't remember seeing him even stand and come over to her. Her eyes weren't closed that long, were they? "Child?" Concern laced his voice. Why was he concerned?

Nessa closed her eyes again. It had been many years since she had actually been sick, and she never remembered it coming on this fast. This was a new feeling. Her stomach cramped, and she felt cold and hot at the same time. She was definitely sick. She needed to get to bed and lie down until it passed. She didn't feel like puking, but just sleeping. Her body was feeling heavy.

"Nessa?" Rolf asked, tapping her face gently.

When Nessa reopened her eyes, he was standing perpendicular to her. That was odd.

"Why did you do that?" Nessa asked of her uncle. She felt sick already; she didn't need him playing jokes on her, too.

There was a hum of a siren going off in the palace. Nessa smiled and wanted to laugh. Devin had to have come through a different gate and set the alarm off. Everything was getting a bit surreal with the ding in the background.

"Do what?" Rolf asked.

"Decided to move sideways," Nessa replied, yawning. "You shouldn't play games on a sick person," she jokingly chastised him. Rolf stared at her, looking confused and worried at the same time.

"Nessa, I didn't move. You're lying down on the couch," Rolf explained as Devin burst through the doorway.

"Turn that stupid noise off," Devin told Rolf, referring to the ding that was still constantly going off every one and three-quarters seconds. Rolf stood and immediately left the room. "Nessa, what is going on?"

Devin picked up Nessa's arm, and she smiled. It was nice that he was going to take care of her when she was sick. Getting a boyfriend proved helpful after all. The pain was fading and she was feeling peaceful. Maybe she was too tired to care about being sick, or maybe she was already getting better. At least Devin was there to watch over her if the pain came back.

"No clue. I feel sick and strange at the same time," she replied and squeezed her eyes shut again. She didn't need her mind to do anything funny with Devin like it had with her uncle.

Devin moved around the room and finally came back to her, but she still didn't open her eyes. She was too tired. It was weird to feel nauseous so quickly, and then suddenly tired. Nessa wasn't too worried, but this was definitely something she had never encountered. His hands were warm as he placed them on her.

"Where does it hurt?" he asked, wiping her forehead as he

waited for a response.

"My stomach was the first place," she replied. "But then everywhere. My feet feel like rocks, and the world is spinning." When Nessa peeked out past her lashes, the world was still warped. It was best to keep her eyes closed. "I felt weird, almost as if I were sick, but I've never felt this way before. It was really bad before you came back. Now I feel fuzzy and tired. Maybe you are magic." Nessa expected a laugh from Devin, but didn't get one in reply. He was genuinely concerned.

"Do you need blood?" Devin asked. Normally a hurt night human could recover with day human blood.

"No, sickness like this can't be cured with blood. I probably just got food poisoning," Nessa replied. Blood was good for a cut on the arm, but not for a bad meal or a cold. "But at this point I wish it could." Nessa felt silly being weak in front of Devin. She really did wish blood would heal her quickly, and then she would be back to normal.

Devin pushed up her shirt, and soon his warm hands were on her stomach. Nessa cringed and smiled at the same time. It was nice to feel his touch, but the situation made it all wrong. His hands on her when she wasn't ill would have been much more ideal. Devin's touch was gentle, but she could feel him moving around. The pain increased as he pushed a little bit, probing her for the problem. Nessa wanted to moan, but kept her mouth shut. She trusted Devin, and knew he wasn't hurting her on purpose. She didn't want to make him feel bad. He was just trying to help.

"I don't know exactly what I'm doing, but my gut tells me to do this," Devin told her.

Nessa peeked out at him from her slightly closed eyes. He was pushing her shirt up further and soon would be exposing more of her flesh than she had yet shown him. Her cheeks would have reddened if they weren't already flaming from the fever that had taken over. As much as she wanted to comment about the shirt staying down, she couldn't even protest; he was trying to heal her. Nessa closed her eyes tighter as his warm touch probed more. He was taking his job healing her very seriously, so she would let it slide that he was getting a bit personal. Again, she wished she was better, and that he was touching her for different reasons.

"I can't feel my hands now," she commented. Her sleepiness made her not worry too much, but the worry from Devin told her that wasn't a good sign. She wasn't sure, but it didn't seem too probable that it was still food poisoning. She had never heard of food poisoning making one go numb before.

Devin's hands prodded her midsection before they began to warm hotter than possible for a day human. He was using magic to heal her. She hadn't expected that. Nessa felt the energy from his hands leave them and go into her body. The warmth entered and swam around inside of her. She felt the tug as the warmness touched every part of her and then came back to where his hands were waiting. He was sending out magic to check over her body internally. She had no clue how he knew to do that, but she was thankful. His touch was soothing, and something about it made everything feel like it would be all right. Devin had that power over her. She felt safe with him even as her body was slowly shutting down.

"I need to make an incision," he warned her as he pressed a cool blade to her hip. She didn't even have time to object before he was making the shallow cut.

Nessa had no clue what he was doing, but she trusted him completely. She had only been to a healer in the village once as a child, and she didn't remember it being like it was with Devin. This was much more personal, and she felt safe, no matter what he told her he planned to do. Devin would do everything in his power to make her feel better. He placed his hand back on her and sent the magic into her veins. The warmth his hands had put into her only moments before was suddenly removed. It was like he was pulling a long string out of every part of her body at once. As it did so, she could feel all of the tingles leave her body. Her strength returned, and she no longer felt sick. He fixed it simply. She waited a moment as the flesh he'd cut healed itself. Slowly, she sat back up. Devin was right there with his free hand on her back, making sure she wasn't still sick. Nessa smiled up at him. He was amazing.

"While that was fun, I'd prefer not to try that again," she told him. She felt much better, but still a bit weak.

Devin made sure that she was stable sitting up before he stood up. Finally, she noticed he was only using one hand to steady her. Hovering between his fingers of his other hand was a greenish-colored blob. He didn't touch it, but it stayed there as if he told it to. He said he didn't know how to use the sidhe magic her grandfather had put in him, but Nessa could see otherwise. Devin was a natural. He took the green liquid and released it in a cup on the table.

"I believe that's the poison you ate." Nessa's mouth dropped open. At no time did she think it was poison. How did he know? How did he remove it? He made it seem easy. "As long as you don't want to feel sick again, I'd stay away from that," Devin advised her as he looked into the cup like he was searching for answers in the green goo.

Nessa remained seated on the floor. Devin finally took his eyes away from the poison long enough to see that she had not moved. He came back and sat beside her, her well-being outweighing his curiosity.

"Are you feeling okay?" he asked as he tenderly took her hand in his.

Nessa felt fine, and Devin felt it, too, through the bond,

but she still couldn't move yet. Someone had tried to kill her with poison, and almost succeeded. What if Devin had not come back that soon? What if there was no Devin, or he didn't have super sidhe powers? Would she be dead now? Nessa never pictured her life ending that easily. It hadn't even occurred to her that she could have been poisoned. Who would stoop to that level? It wasn't common to kill sidhe with poison. Assassins would use poison as a backup, like a blade covered in it, but it was never used alone. That wasn't the way of the sidhe. It was strange and unheard of in all of Nessa's time living here. She was trained as a warrior, and always thought the end would come fighting, not lying paralyzed due to poison. Reality hit hard, and she couldn't move from her spot.

Anger and concern pulsed through the bond. Devin was a mixture of emotion over the situation, and the sight of her not back to complete health seemed to make him even angrier. Nessa could feel his power pulsating from him, but she couldn't even speak to tell him to calm down. She still couldn't completely grasp what he had just told her. Someone had poisoned her.

Devin stood back up, and walked a circle around the room to calm himself before squatting down to pick her up in his arms. He carried her through the sitting room and into the bedroom. Gently, he laid her on the sheets and grabbed a blanket at the end of the bed to cover her. Nessa was still too shocked by the events. He stroked the side of her face while gazing into her eyes. Nessa could feel him in her mind, looking for what was wrong. She didn't have the willpower to hide it from him.

Suddenly, the world around Nessa had just become a bit more real. Before, it had been easy to ignore everything going on. She was always hidden away from the sidhe world due to her own solitary ways, or her brother keeping her out of it. She had heard of things, she had even seen the dead from all of the fighting that went on between the clans, but she'd never felt she was part of it. Even after returning home, Devin kept her completely safe and isolated from the truth. In that moment, she realized that she was no longer isolated. In fact, she was going to be king of the hill in a few days, and everyone would be trying to knock her down.

"I'm sorry," Devin told her, lying down beside her and taking her into his arms. He had seen enough to know what bothered her. "I should have been here. I won't make the same mistake again. I promise you that you are safe. I'll make sure of that."

Nessa shook her head no. That was the problem. Even if Devin had been there, nothing would have happened differently. He could save her from invisible assassins, but there was no way he could save her from poison every time. Yet Devin was sure that he could. Nessa wanted to believe that it wasn't just words, but it was too hard to wrap her mind around what had happened.

Nessa gently rested her face against his chest. She felt safe in his arms, yet her world had been shattered. Was she ever going to be safe? Was it even possible to keep her safe? Devin had promised her, but there was only so much that he could do. Nessa didn't want to think anymore, so she let the sleep that was edging at her consciousness take her. Blackness was a comfort compared to what her world had just become.

Devin slipped his arm out from beneath Nessa once he was sure she was asleep again. She might have felt better from the poison getting out of her system and regaining much of her strength, but she was still tired. Devin looked to the assassins standing just outside of the doorway. They could protect her physically, but what could they do against poison? The palace wasn't safe as far as Devin was concerned. He had to figure out where the poison came from and if he could stop it. He needed to right Nessa's world. Devin wanted her to feel safe, and he needed the sidhe to stop playing games. Standing by and letting them harm her again wasn't an option. She hadn't done a single thing to deserve the hate she was receiving from them.

"No one comes in or out of here until I get back," he ordered the assassins. All four nodded. Nessa would be safe if she stayed right where she was, and no one was allowed to get close to her with poison again.

Devin left Nessa's rooms and went straight to the kitchen. He had no doubts from her descriptions of pain that the food was poisoned. Most of the poison he found in her was concentrated around her stomach anyways. He didn't even pay attention to the shocked sidhe that scampered away from him as soon as they saw him. He needed to find the source of the poison, and possibly the culprit if he were lucky. This had to end. The elite sidhe feared him, so he didn't understand why this was happening. Who was that arrogant that they would go against him? Was that why they turned to poison? Would it be hard to find the person?

Pushing open the large wooden door, Devin stepped into the steaming kitchen. Food preparation was constantly going on all day for the palace. Cooks ran from place to place as some chopped, stirred, and even cleaned vegetables. No one noticed when he entered since they each all at their jobs diligently.

"Who is in charge?" Devin asked the closest person.

The young girl's eyes went wide at the sight of him, and she mouthed a reply that had no sound behind it. Her finger pointed to a portly woman who was beating bread dough into submission. Devin walked over but didn't say anything as the lady worked. As she finished with the loaf she was working on, he glanced around the room. However, he couldn't feel a trace of the poison anywhere in the kitchen.

The cook finally looked up and jumped a little at the sight of him. Quickly, she curtsied to cover up her astonishment, and waited for him to speak.

"Were you the one to prepare the morning meals?" Devin asked.

"I supervise all meal preparations," she replied proudly, but with a hint of fear. Devin couldn't decipher if the fear was from him, or something she had done.

"Were there any new people in the kitchen today?" Devin asked. The cook wouldn't be prideful if she were the one that had done it.

"No, just my regulars," she replied. She answered as quick and short as she could. Her eyes darted around the room as Devin watched her. She was still afraid of him, but she was dedicated to her job.

"Can you get everyone that was working this morning to line up here?" he asked, pointing next to him. It was going to make meal preparations halt, but Devin didn't care. He needed to find the poison and poisoner.

The cook nodded and began calling to several of the people working around the large kitchen. They all moved promptly at her voice and formed a line in front of him. The cook didn't even question Devin. She gave orders, and seemed to follow them just as dedicatedly. Devin looked from scared face to scared face.

"Do you know who I am?" Devin asked, and all gathered quickly nodded their heads. "And you know that I can tell if you are lying?" The heads rattled again. The former king was legendary. Even the young women before him who had never met the king knew what his powers were like. Everyone knew that Devin now had those powers. He wasn't completely sure how to turn on and off the lie detecting abilities, but everyone feared him, so he was fairly certain they would tell him the truth even if it didn't work.

"Can I ask what the problem is, sir?" the cook asked as her workers all trembled in fear. She was braver than the rest for sure.

"The future queen was poisoned this morning. It was in her food," Devin replied curtly. "Food that was made here, in the kitchen."

Gasps around the room were heard as everyone stopped working to watch the commotion Devin was causing. It wasn't just the line of women before him that heard his declaration. He didn't like being a show, but he needed answers. The kitchen was now quiet—except for the sizzle of cooking food—so it was going to be easier to speak to them.

"Is she alive?" the young girl, who couldn't speak at the sight of him before, asked from behind Devin. He was happy to find that at least one person was concerned for Nessa.

"Yes, she is," Devin replied, and looked over the line of women standing before him. All were shaking in their boots, but that was the same as before he had announced what he knew. Nothing had changed.

Devin moved in front of the first girl. "Did you poison the food?" he asked.

She stared at the floor and shook her head vehemently. *No.* Devin pushed her face up to view her eyes.

"I need a verbal reply," he told her. He knew enough about the power to realize that he needed them to speak. It had something to do with the tone of their voice that gave all lies away.

"No," she squeaked out. Devin could see that she was telling the truth.

Devin moved down the line to each of the girls. They were all innocent. As he stopped in front of the cook, he looked to her. She was the last one left to ask. He doubted she was involved, but he sensed that everyone else was innocent. Who else was left?

"Don't even think of asking me," the cook replied. "I have been working here my whole life. Keeping the nobles fed and happy has been a lifelong goal. I'd never hurt a single one, and certainly not Miss Nessa. She's the kindest of the bunch," the cook replied. She was truthful, too. Another sidhe that was on Nessa's side was reassuring, but that still didn't answer his plight. Who could it be? Devin was sure that it had been in the food. Was he wrong?

Devin nodded and moved to walk away to inspect the room. He looked around, but kept watch on the line of cooks. It didn't add up. When the cook reached up and wiped her forehead with a rag that hung from her waist, it hit Devin. He could feel the poison now that he'd removed it from Nessa, and he'd just felt the warm tug of the poison on the rag. Quickly, he stopped the cook from moving the rag closer to her face. He was near enough, and fast enough, that the rag didn't make it to the skin. His sudden movement startled the cook.

"Everyone turn their hands over," he said, looking around the room. He realized he was right. He could feel the poison everywhere. Minute pieces of it were on almost every person. The room was filled with the poison. They were lucky no one had died there yet. "No one move," Devin ordered the shocked women. They obeyed him.

He closed his eyes and concentrated. The warmth of his hands expanded in the already hot space. He needed to get the poison out of the kitchen, or more people would die from it. He searched for the poison and drew it from all of the corners of the room. It pulled to him, and it solidified a mass in his hands. He had no clue how he did it, but it was happening. He kept the liquid ball suspended above his hands as he finished cleaning the room. All of the poison was with him now. Carefully keeping it suspended, he turned back to the cooks in the room.

"The poison was in here, and most of you have touched it. I believe none of you had anything to do with it, but from now on, Cook, don't let anyone in the kitchen that isn't here right now," Devin ordered. She nodded, still shocked by the poison hovering above Devin's hand. She was close to having ingested it herself. When her shock wore off, she hurried over to a cupboard and got Devin a vial with a lid to put the poison inside of. Step one of finding the poison was successful, but he was nowhere near close to finding out who had done it. He could call the usual suspects, but each family wanted Nessa dead now. He'd have more than enough people to search through and he needed to narrow it down, but was unsure of how to do it.

'Devin, Bray O'Ryan is dead,' Nessa told Devin urgently through their bond.

The sidhe were back to killing each other. Now Devin was unsure if Bray had been the target or Nessa, but it didn't matter. Devin had told them no assassins, but he wasn't clear enough. He should have said no assassinations. Nessa McKinny didn't seem to be the only target of this poison, and the sidhe were back to their old ways. Devin needed to be sure they understood what he had meant.

CHAPTER 3

Nessa stood over the dead body of the man that had accused her of premeditated murder only a day ago. Bray O'Ryan thought he could get Nessa dethroned before she could actually take it, but that had ended when they returned from the crypt with her grandfather's powers. In reality it wasn't Bray that had accused her, but rather his likeness. His grandson, disguised as him, was running the farce of a trial. It was still eerie to look at the man dead, even if she hadn't really known him well.

"You can't come in here. This is the O'Ryan wing, and neither of you are welcome here. We don't like traitors who kill their king," Owen O'Ryan, Bray's grandson, stated. He was still set against Nessa, even though there was no way to keep her off the throne now. "Besides, you probably did this to him. This is a girl's way of killing—poison. You're the only girl I know that would have a grudge against us."

Devin glared at the younger man. He was testing Devin's patience, and Nessa didn't know how much Devin would take before he did something. Owen had caused them enough grief already. It wasn't like they wanted to be there. Neither Devin nor Nessa really wanted to see Bray after what he and his grandson had put Nessa through. If they didn't need more answers about the poison and poisoner, they probably would have avoided seeing the old man.

"Nessa was poisoned this morning as well. I doubt she'd poison herself, too, if it were her," Devin replied, stooping down to take a closer look at the old man. He was still warm, and there was nothing that one could see as physically wrong with him. Devin was being good about keeping his anger at Owen inside himself, but Nessa could feel it right beneath the surface.

"If it wasn't her, then it must have been the Miller family. We killed one of the nephews of the lead Miller a month ago. Without assassins he must have sent one of the women. This is how they retaliate," Owen replied, who was obviously still caught up on blaming women because it was a poison. Nessa would have much rather put a blade through his neck. Did that not make her a girl?

Two men dressed all in white entered the room. They looked to Owen, and then to Devin, before they examined the old man. Nessa moved out of the way, as they were the collectors that came to take dead bodies.

'They're here for the dead man,' Nessa explained to Devin quickly since he didn't move. Nessa was beginning to forget that there was so much of the sidhe village that Devin still didn't know.

"We need to prepare the body for interment," one of the men stated quietly, explaining what Nessa had already told him through the bond.

Devin nodded and stood up. When the white-robed men began to wash the dead man, Devin walked a few steps away, and Nessa stayed right at his side. The air in the room was charged. Owen was upset about his grandfather, and he didn't seem to believe Devin that Nessa wasn't involved. Owen had already proven unpredictable, and Nessa wasn't sure Devin would let him live if he refused to cooperate. It was best for her to keep close to Devin at that point.

"What exactly happened?" Devin asked Owen, being direct and to the point.

Owen looked startled by the question, but did reply. "I went and got food this morning. I brought it up, but grandfather had said he was hungry, too. I gave him my tray and went back for more. When I returned, I found him lying right there. He was still alive at that point, but he couldn't move and told me he wanted to sleep."

"And you didn't call for anyone?" Devin asked, a bit suspicious, but Owen didn't seem to catch what Devin was really insinuating.

"We take care of our own families. I know a few things, and I figured it was something I could handle," Owen replied, his hubris showing through.

Devin nodded and watched the men preparing the body. Nessa looked to the men, also. She had seen the ritual several times before, so it was nothing new to her, but she was trying to see what Devin was searching for. The collectors were from each family, and these were the O'Ryan collectors. They were basically the same, but none of the families shared or interacted with them. Nessa knew part of the reason Owen was upset that Devin and she were there was that he didn't want her to see how they handled the body. They would prepare the body to be put into the crypt. In general, after they bathed the body they would cast spells on it to preserve it for one year. Those spells were sacred and unique to each family. Nessa didn't care about the spells. She cared about the poison and wondered what Devin was analyzing.

"What were his symptoms?" Devin asked, pulling his eyes from the men handling the body.

"He complained that he was cold, and it was quickly done. When it happened like that, I knew I couldn't help him and stood to call for my father. Before I could even find someone else, he was dead," Owen explained. Nessa shivered. She might not have had much more time if Devin hadn't been there. "It was that quick."

Devin nodded, again analyzing the body. Nessa was constantly amazed by how much Devin understood and could get from just small conversations. She was thankful that he was around. He would make her life easier and maybe, just maybe, the sidhe needed someone like him. They might not agree, but Nessa could see it. Devin was unique, and the sidhe had a lot to learn.

"Is that the food he was eating?" Devin asked. Nessa had noticed the half-eaten food, too.

"No, that's mine. I don't know where my grandfather's food went," Owen replied, a little shocked as he glanced around the room as well. How could a tray of food disappear?

What does that mean?' Nessa asked Devin, who began to look around the spacious sitting room. He wasn't as baffled by the news as she was.

Someone knew we would look at the food. I went to the kitchen earlier. I didn't find any food contaminated there either,' Devin replied. *Someone is very good at covering their tracks.'*

What if it isn't the same poison?' Nessa asked. It could have just been a coincidence that they were all poisoned on the same day. While unlikely, hers could have been different. They had no way to know.

Devin stared down at the dead body; Nessa had made a good point.

"What are they doing?" Devin asked both Nessa and Owen. The robed men had moved on in their preparations, and a faint spell had been cast above the dead man's feet.

"They are enchanting his body to make it last for one year to put in the crypt. We celebrate the death of a sidhe with an after year of viewing and remembering. They make it so he doesn't decay as he lies in the crypt," Nessa explained. She had shown Devin the crypt extensively, but she wasn't sure why it was relevant now.

'Make them stop,' Devin ordered as he stooped down next to the upper half of Bray's body.

Nessa wanted to snap at him that she wasn't his secretary, but his tone of voice told her that she shouldn't. She didn't understand, but listened to Devin anyway. "Stop now," Nessa said, commanding the men to stop.

Owen began to protest before noticing Devin by his grandfather's head, and he immediately positioned himself to take his grandfather away from Devin.

"Don't touch him, day human." Owen snarled, moving to attack Devin. However, Devin didn't even flinch as he continued to check the man for poison.

'The poison is stuck where they already preserved him for his after year. I won't be able to get it out if they continue,' Devin told Nessa. Her anger at his direct commands lessened as he explained. Nessa had been trying to give Devin more of a chance since she found out he actually loved her, but it was hard. Everything inside of her told her to fight back when he was brash. *'I think there's enough not fixed to get a sample. It might be small, but you're right. We do need to see if it's the same poison. We need to know if this is just one group or if there are others also acting with poison.'*

That made sense. Even Nessa was unsure how the sidhe would react to not being able to use assassins. Would they all turn to poison, since Devin had banned the assassins? They needed the poison to examine it, and Owen needed to back off. Nessa prepared herself to fight if Owen tried anything.

Owen jumped at Devin as he conversed silently with Nessa, and she leapt at the approaching sidhe. She defensively stood in front of Devin, and waited for the fury of the younger O'Ryan.

Owen wasn't going to attack Devin while he worked. Nessa would be sure of that. She may not have liked Devin's tone in ordering her around, but he was still her bonded human. Nessa glared at Owen, waiting for him to move, but nothing came. As Owen jumped, he seemed to bounce right off an invisible shield which was surrounding Devin and Nessa. Owen hit the floor with a crash and Nessa stood back up.

'What is that?' Nessa asked Devin. She didn't feel anything around them.

'Protection,' Devin replied, standing with a small bubble of poison above his hand. "They may finish now," Devin told Nessa.

Nessa nodded to the men who were waiting and watching the scene. No matter what Owen said or did, Nessa was their future queen, and they were not going to move without Nessa's orders. Owen stood up from where he landed on the floor ungracefully.

"What is that?" Owen asked, pointing to Devin's hand and accusing Devin with his eyes of doing something evil to his dead grandfather.

"The poison," Nessa replied, rolling her own eyes at Owen. He was just trying to pick a fight. Owen was the prime example why Nessa couldn't stand most of the elite sidhe; they were all like him. "And now we just need to find out who sent it to you."

Although Nessa didn't need to explain more, she was upset that the sidhe thought that by being an outsider Devin was doing something bad or evil. Devin was the only one in the palace, beyond her own cousins, that had no agenda to sabotage a single person. Even after Maureen, one of the elders, sent her son after Nessa, Devin wasn't looking for revenge.

Owen stayed by his grandfather's body as he glared at Devin. Nessa was unsure what the glare was for, but guessed that he didn't like being bested by an invisible shield. Nessa had to try to keep a serious face. She had no idea why the sidhe kept underestimating Devin even after he received her grandfather's powers. Their attempts were fruitless even before he had them. They stood no chance now.

"There's only one place to look," Owen said, very sure of himself and his assessment. "The Millers did this." Owen stood, waiting for a reply of agreement.

Devin turned to look at Owen. The O'Ryan heir was still mad at Devin, but he was back to his cocky self. His ego didn't seem to stay bruised. Devin shook his head, and even Nessa found Owen a bit much to handle.

"If that's true, why did they poison two of their own this morning along with you?" Devin revealed.

Owen opened his mouth to reply, but didn't have one. Even Nessa was shocked by the news. Devin took her hand in his—the one that wasn't holding the poison—and walked her back to her room. He kept his thoughts to himself even though she could have eavesdropped into them. Devin was already trying to figure out the puzzle.

"How did you know?" Nessa asked as they approached her apartment.

Devin dropped her hand to open the door and grinned.

"I heard the healers mention they already had done two bodies over at the Miller's wing today when they entered the room." Devin motioned for Nessa to go forward.

Nessa shook her head. That was the best part of people ignoring day humans. If they didn't run in fear, they tended to be careless around him. And Devin, being Devin, would always use that to his advantage. He was just what the sidhe needed.

The auditorium filled quickly with the elite sidhe families. Devin had to make only one demand to get them to meet him in the large room, and they arrived in fear. Those that knew the old king feared what Devin could do, and those that did not know feared what they saw in their elder's eyes. Even after their rough treatment, Devin had waited as patiently as he could for the sidhe to remove their dead to the crypt before announcing to all of them to meet him in the auditorium. That didn't mean he was in a good mood. He was fuming from the assassinations and the attempt on Nessa's life. Devin had specifically told them to stop killing each other with assassins. He had meant the "stop killing" part as the emphasis, but the sidhe took it that the hidden assassins were the problem. They didn't see the wrong behind the continuous killing. Devin needed to make them stop, and had to figure out how to change the way they saw the world. Not too big of a task.

The sidhe were gathered together so that Devin could see each and every one of them. He needed to look into the faces of the elite sidhe to tell who was lying. Someone had ordered a hit on the people who were killed. Three families had been attacked. It was likely one of the two families left had planned it, but he wasn't completely sure. He didn't put it past the sidhe, who had no problems killing people left and right, to kill their own family to hide themselves. Who would go against his demand that they stop the assassinations, though? He wasn't just figuring it out to save Nessa. The elite sidhe were killing each other off. Didn't they see that at the rate they were going, it would lead to everyone ending up dead?

Devin could sense the elite in the auditorium waiting for him to arrive. He needed to take his time. His temper was getting the better of him now that the adrenalin had worn off from his rush to save Nessa. The feelings he felt for Nessa were new. Devin was used to being able to control all of his emotions. Even when he found himself in love with his last charge, he still was able to keep it at bay and do his job. Unfortunately, it wasn't that easy with Nessa. More and more, he found that he was losing control. He wasn't sure how Nessa could get him bothered, but he was upset about what happened. Devin felt responsible for leaving her behind, and not being there as soon as she fell sick. He wasn't going to make that mistake again. He would protect Nessa … no matter what.

Devin thoroughly looked around the palace to see where each sidhe was, and discovered they were all waiting in the auditorium for him. It was time to go interrogate the elite. Nessa was safe sitting in the room with him, but he had to be sure she would stay safe. He needed to be the monster sidhe that the old king had made him. It was time to get the elite to fall in line with his demands. When Devin stood and walked to the doorway of Nessa's apartment, she followed.

"Not you," Devin said to her without turning around to face her. He couldn't let her go there where she could be a target.

"What?" Nessa asked, shocked by his statement, and upset that he was acting bossy again.

"There is no *what*," Devin replied. "Someone in that room tried to kill you and several others today. I do not want you there. It isn't safe." He couldn't make it any clearer.

Nessa stared at him, unable to respond. Nodding as if the conversation was done, Devin opened the door. Since Devin could feel every sidhe and no one was near her, he knew she was safe alone in her room. He needed her to stay safe so that he could concentrate on what he needed to do.

"You can't just keep me locked in my room," Nessa replied, anger rising. She obviously didn't like the situation, which Devin could understand, but his need to protect her ruled over his empathy. "I'm a big girl, after all."

Devin didn't even respond. He just walked away. Nessa tried to follow, but the room was surrounded by the same invisible barrier he had accidentally used before. He was happy that he'd learned the trick, even if it was because of stress, and knew she wouldn't be getting out. Devin heard her exasperated scream as he walked away, but he didn't care. He'd already left her unprotected today, and he wanted nothing except to keep her safe, so he wasn't letting her walk into a room full of sidhe ready to kill her.

'If you don't come back right now, I'm never going to talk to you again,' she threatened when she found screaming didn't work.

Turning, Devin gazed at her. She was obviously unhappy that she was stuck in her room, and he had to fight not to go back and take her hand in his. He wanted her to be happy, but more so he needed her to be safe. She meant too much to him to endanger her. He just shook his head before turning back around.

'I mean it,' she yelled through their connection. However, he didn't even miss a step as he walked down the hall, in the direction of the auditorium.

When he finally arrived, there was no one left to wait for, so he could start immediately. He needed to get it over with quickly before Nessa got too mad. Rolf—the only elite that Devin trusted to tell him the truth about the rules of the sidhe world when he needed it—waited by the door as asked, and escorted him to the front of the room. Devin stood before the sidhe and looked from each family head to the next as the room quieted.

"Today we face the task of burying three people. They were all killed by poison," Devin began. No one spoke; everyone knew what had happened by now. "I had told you before that there would be no more assassinations. I can tell that someone didn't exactly understand what I was saying. I meant for you to stop killing each other. You are all too blind with hatred to see what you are doing. If you kill each other off, *yes,* someone will be left standing, but what will they rule? There will be no one left. This needs to stop, and it stops now. If there's a grievance, it needs to be settled in the courts, not with the death of someone."

The sidhe stared blankly at Devin. Most didn't grasp what he was saying, or understand how serious he was. It was a concept they couldn't comprehend. Devin searched the faces of the younger sidhe first, and discovered they were defiant to his words. He glanced around some more. The old sidhe were wary of him in general. His message wasn't getting through.

"If I find anyone is responsible for the killings today, or any day in the future, I'll remove their entire family from the noble class of sidhe. You will all be required to go back and live with the common sidhe. If I find that the heads of the family ..." Devin looked specifically at Maureen—the lady Nessa thought was her adoptive mother figure in her life, but in reality, she was the one trying to get her killed any way possible. "If it is the head of a family, they will not just be removed from their noble status. The head of the family, along with direct descendants, will be kicked out of the village permanently."

A collective gasp was heard throughout the room as they finally understood how serious he was, and Devin had to hide the smirk that was forming on his face. It took drastic measures to get through to them, and he'd hit the nail on the head when he figured out the most important thing to these people was their status. They had such little care for life, but their noble status meant everything. He was angry when he entered the room, but to be able to shock them all with the prospect of being kicked out made him smile. Devin had come to the sidhe without a real home left, knew what it was like to contemplate starting over, but it didn't scare him like he visibly saw in the sidhe now. They truly feared not being nobles, or not living in the village. Devin couldn't understand this, as he saw the sidhe people as strong and resilient. After all, they had managed to keep their own culture, yet now he wondered if maybe it wasn't strength, but rather fear, that kept them going. Maybe the thought of exile was just what they needed to inspire them to stop killing each other off.

'*What did you do now?*' Nessa asked in Devin's head. She felt the chaos falling off all of the sidhe in the room. They were even more scared of him now, if that was possible.

'*I see we are talking now. Forever came quickly,*' Devin replied.

He looked around the room one last time before leaving. His message had been received. Whoever did this wasn't going to have help, nor would they willing admit it. Hopefully Devin's threat would keep the chaos limited to the one assassin that they were looking for, and no one would think to join them.

Silence was Nessa's reply to Devin's comment. He was sure there would be silence the rest of the day, but he knew Nessa well enough by now. She wouldn't stay quiet for long. It wasn't in her to do that. At that moment, he didn't care if she was mad at him. She was safe, and that was all that mattered. She'd forgive him soon enough.

After Devin's meeting with the sidhe the day before, Nessa wasn't thrilled to be waking the next night and having to deal with the fallout. She'd found out from her uncle that Devin—being as overprotective as he always was—told the sidhe that if they continued to put out assassinations, he would disband any family that was involved. Nessa would have told him that wasn't a tactic that would work with the sidhe, but he was too angry to listen, and she was too angry to help him out. The sidhe would never let another family be made into commoners, but who knew. Devin did seem to have a way to make what he wanted to happen, happen.

Rolf was early, like the day before, and Nessa was surprised to wake and find that Devin was actually in the room with her. He had already gotten breakfast, and had a tray waiting for her. She continued being mad at him for essentially locking her in her own room, and refused to eat what he'd brought. She didn't fear the food, as Devin would make sure it was safe, but she needed to make a point. Devin couldn't just lock her away like a helpless princess. Nessa was anything but helpless. When Rolf knocked, she was grateful to get away from Devin before she caved. It was much harder to stay mad at him now that she knew everything through the bond. He wasn't even doing this to be mean. In fact, he was being more than caring, and she hated that she could feel it. Since his emotions were something new to her, she didn't know how to block them out of her mind, and now he was freely sharing. He was worried beyond belief about her. She'd never had someone worried about her safety before, not even her family. It was all new and strange. As she opened the door for her waiting uncle, she had to hide her smile. Nessa wasn't going to let Devin win, even if he truly was trying to keep her safe and happy.

"Did you look over the list?" Rolf asked, tentatively glancing into the room. Rolf was back to fearing Devin now that his worry over Nessa had passed.

Devin nodded to Rolf, and Nessa saw the small shiver that Rolf had in reply. At least one sidhe took Devin seriously, not that Uncle Rolf would have had anything to do with her assassination attempt. Her family gained nothing by her death, as her cousin and Rolf's son had already made it clear that he wouldn't take the throne. Since there was no one left in direct line from her grandfather to take the throne, Rolf supported her completely.

"I figured that list is too long," Devin answered, joining Nessa at the doorway. Because he was standing so close to her, Nessa could feel the heat coming off of him.

"It is one of the requirements," Rolf squeaked out, "to take the throne."

"I'm not trying to change tradition," Devin replied kindly. He had to have seen his effect on Rolf, but he didn't comment on it. "I was thinking that if Nessa took the elite sidhe complaints, and I took the commoner complaints, it could be done possibly in a day instead of dragging out right up until the moment of the coronation. I know she must decide on the cases, as her word will be law, but I'm bonded to her, and have both her and her grandfather's blood running through me now. I figured I could just be an extension of her."

Rolf's mouth hung open, and Nessa had to cough to hide her smile. She wasn't sure Uncle Rolf had even considered that Devin would offer to help, neither had she, and Devin did have a point. He was always prepared. There was no reason he couldn't be an extension of Nessa.

"I suppose that will work," Rolf replied, finally coming to his senses.

Devin took the lists Rolf had given Nessa the day before and handed one to Nessa, keeping the second for himself. Nessa focused on the paper in her hand as he tried to catch her attention with a smile. At any time he could mentally talk to her, but he was giving her some space. Nessa wanted to be angry that he could act so perfectly, but she was rapidly losing the battle.

"Then we should get started," Devin replied, motioning for Rolf to lead the way.

Rolf began to walk down the hallway, and Devin stayed

behind Nessa, waiting for her to follow her uncle. Planning, helping, and even being courteous. What more could Nessa wish for in a guy? Devin was the complete package.

'Why?' Nessa asked silently without turning around. She was too close to caving in and forgiving him for being overprotective.

'Why what, princess?' Devin replied innocently.

'Why listen to grievances?' Nessa began to walk after her uncle. Devin kept in step behind her, which Nessa appreciated since she wouldn't have to turn around and look at him.

'Why not? Did you see the list? You'd be in there from sundown to sunup every moment until the coronation. I figure if I help out, you might just get a bit of rest. You did almost die yesterday,' Devin replied. She didn't need to be reminded, but she felt it again. He was taking the poisoning upon himself again, thinking it was his fault. Nessa shook off the feeling.

His reply made sense, but Nessa still didn't completely understand. Why would he spend time listening to people complain? That didn't sound like fun. None of the other rulers ever had help. Her brother, Rhys, had ruled on his own. Her father never asked her mother to help with anything. Her grandfather ruled with an iron fist that no one could deny. They sat for hours listening to complaints from common and elite sidhe alike. It kind of went with the job, no matter how boring it could be. Devin was a strange addition to the sidhe world, and she would have to get used to that fact.

Rolf stopped at the amphitheater and looked between Devin and Nessa.

"If you both are to be meeting with people, we will need a second room," Rolf told them, aware that his logistics wouldn't work well.

"I can meet with the common sidhe in the courtyard," Devin replied. That was so Devin. He didn't require a fancy room where he sat above the people. A park bench in the courtyard was more than enough for him. Nessa knew exactly why the sidhe needed Devin as their king: they needed the humility that went with the man she fell in love with.

"If you would like," Rolf replied, perplexed by the arrangement. He couldn't fathom why Devin would want to sit as equals with commoners.

Nessa shook her head as she caught Devin's innocent glance at her. He knew exactly why Rolf was confused. All of the sidhe were confused by Devin, and that was a good thing. Since he was being himself, he didn't mind in the least.

"Once Nessa is settled, I'll wait in the east courtyard for anyone on the commoner list," Devin explained as he ushered Rolf and Nessa into the large room in which he'd threatened the noble sidhe just the day before.

Nessa followed her uncle past the waiting mob of people without looking to see who was there. The list said enough. At least a quarter, maybe even half of the palace residents had a complaint. They usually settled grudges themselves, therefore she knew there wasn't going to be much with real substance. It was going to be a long day, and she wasn't looking forward to any of it. However, since Devin had cut her list in half, it wasn't going to be as bad as she'd originally thought when Rolf had handed her the list. At least she hoped it wouldn't be as bad.

Nessa tentatively sat down in the ornate chair in the front of the room. It was ridiculous to be up on display, and never in her life had she thought she'd be there. This was her father's seat, Rhys's seat ... she wasn't the heir. Unfortunately, she was the only one left. Reality was settling in. While she still couldn't fathom the coronation that would occur in less than two days, this made things a bit more real.

'I'll be back when I am done,' Devin told her, leaning down

to kiss her cheek before leaving. *'All four of the assassins are with you, but if anything at all seems strange, call for me.'*

He was still worried. Nessa watched him walk out of the room, and noted how all of the sidhe sitting around shied away as he passed. Nessa had always wondered why her grandfather never remarried after his wife died, or why he'd never had friends. It was a bit clearer now: with great power came fear and loneliness. The elite were showing that Devin would never find a friend in their crowd, and they would never stop fearing him.

Rolf walked up near Nessa and bent down to whisper in her ear. He stopped abruptly about a foot away from her face, startled, but trying not to show it. Nessa was confused and reached up to touch her uncle, but something stopped her. Her hand hit an invisible wall. She was safely encased, kept away from everyone, even her harmless uncle.

Nessa huffed. She thought Devin was being a gentleman by offering to return to walk back with her to their rooms, but now she saw the truth. He had placed his protective bubble around her, and she was stuck sitting in that chair until he returned. He was going overboard. Four invisible assassins and a protective bubble no one could enter. Nessa was beyond safe … she was a captive. Her anger returned. It was one thing to be protective, but Devin was a bit obsessive. That was going to have to change.

CHAPTER 4

Devin finished the last person on his list about midway through the night. It was simple to listen to the common sidhe because they had real disputes that had easy answers. There was no trickery or lies, and everything was straight forward. One sidhe had been providing clay for the potter, yet the potter wasn't returning the favor by giving the pottery he said he would.

Devin could relate to the common sidhe; with them he saw something worth saving. The elite would have driven him nuts. Everything about them was petty and filled with lies. Due to her upbringing, Nessa was way more suited to dealing with them.

Slowly, Devin stood and stretched. There was still time to go for a walk through the town. He wanted to learn more about the common sidhe since he had sat in on all of the cases. He learned new facts with each case, and now pictured the village differently. They were beginning to mean more to him, feel real to him, and he couldn't help his curiosity. He wanted to see everything.

Unfortunately, that would have to wait. Nessa had already figured out that he had placed her in protective bubble she couldn't move from, and he could feel her anger across the bond. It wasn't his intention to make her mad, he just wanted her safe, and it was the only solution he could come up with quickly when he saw the amount of nobles in the room. They were scared when he was around, but he was sure once he had left they would all be looking for a way to get rid of Nessa. He could feel the emotions behind each person. Fear was foremost, but there was also disgust upon seeing Nessa. Not a single person that sat there with a grievance wanted a female leader. Devin didn't know how they would act without him around, and therefore had done what he felt he must.

Devin waited until the last commoner had been escorted out of the palace courtyard before he stood to join Nessa … just not inside of her room. She had to have more cases left, since she had more people to see to begin with, but he would wait outside nonetheless. Devin peeked in the room, but that was as far as he planned to go until she was done.

Nessa was still seated in the front of the room—it wasn't like she could move, after all—and Devin paused to watch her. She was listening to a case presented to her by an older man, and her concentration was completely focused on what he was saying. She didn't notice Devin enter the room, and she wasn't paying attention to the waiting sidhe. She was actually listening in order to make a good choice in the matter. She cared. Devin was unsure how she did it. The elite sidhe drove him nuts, but she was there making each person feel like what they had to say was important. She was a light in the dark world of the elite sidhe, and Devin felt unworthy to be beside her. He would do whatever he could to keep her safe, even if it made her mad. Devin was meant to be behind the scenes, protecting people, and he would do everything to let her be the light they needed. The old king might have told Devin he was there to save the sidhe, but in reality, Nessa needed to be the one to do it. Devin was still in shock that she was his and would be forever. He couldn't hide the love that crossed the bond. She was amazing.

As Nessa sat listening, Devin watched her, and couldn't

help but think that she was smart and beautiful. She had considered everything about the man's plea carefully. The older man nodded and walked back to his seat after her decision, and immediately the next person stood and walked forward. She had more to listen to. Devin moved to hide behind the door, but stopped. He could only see the back of the next petitioner's head, but from Nessa's face he had to guess she knew the woman. This wasn't going to go well.

"I'd like to present my plea that you step down as future queen and back your nephew as the next heir to the throne," Maureen stated loud enough for everyone in the room to be witness to. Nessa had no nephews. Rhys was her only sibling, and he died unmarried and childless.

Devin felt his stomach drop, or maybe it was Nessa's stomach. They were too connected by now to know which one was more shocked. Devin knew about Fiona, but he had yet to tell Nessa, or even process what it meant when he'd found out she was pregnant. Yes, he thought it could be a problem, but he also didn't think they'd deal with it until after the baby was born.

Nessa's eyes flew to Devin at the back of the room. She'd known he was there and had been watching.

'What is she talking about?' Nessa asked Devin, since he wasn't as shocked as she was.

Devin cringed. Fiona was seated next to her mother, and stood to join her. Fiona's protruding belly answered the question. It was too late to just stand and watch the cases. Devin needed to step in with the fear he had created, and stop the farce before Maureen got anyone to actually join her side. The last thing the sidhe needed was to be divided.

Devin brushed off the shock that Maureen would be that blunt and hurried down to the stage. Rolf's mouth was still hanging open, like most others in the room. Fiona hadn't just hid her pregnancy from Nessa and Devin, but from everyone. Even after they'd dropped their illusions, she was still able to hide it, but was making no effort now to hide her belly.

Nessa was confused by it all, and couldn't take her eyes off Fiona until Devin was next to her. He nodded to Nessa, taking a place beside her. Nessa was prepared to deal with the elite sidhe seeking help and answers, but she wasn't prepared to deal with the likes of Maureen. The older woman was cunning, and had tried on several occasions to take the throne; first through her daughter and Rhys, then through Nessa and her now dead son Finn, and finally through a grandchild that was obviously going to arrive soon. No one was prepared to face Maureen, and that was just the way the old lady liked it. Maureen grinned at Nessa and Devin happily.

"Rhys was never married," Nessa finally spoke. Devin hid his smile. Maybe Nessa was prepared to deal with Maureen.

"He has no legitimate heir," Rolf replied, joining in on the decision. "The law states only legitimate heirs can rule. Besides, for all we know, Rhys may not be the father." Rolf was quick to Nessa's aid. He knew, as well as Devin, that no one wanted Maureen in power but Maureen. The old lady was ruthless and had a heart of stone. The sidhe were doing a good enough job killing each other off on their own. With Maureen in charge there would be no hope to save the sidhe.

"My daughter only had been with King Rhys. She was a virgin before she met him, and now she is pregnant. It's his child," Maureen replied. Devin glanced at Fiona. Did she appreciate her private life being divulged for the sake of the argument her mom was making? Ever the dutiful child, Fiona was a statue beside her mother, so Devin couldn't tell. "I have hundreds of witnesses that would tell you Fiona and Rhys were together. They were even secretly married," Maureen added, and the room erupted in talk.

Devin stared at Maureen. She was lying, but he had no proof, just as she had no proof. It was word against word. Sidhe against day human. There was no weight behind his words without being a true sidhe, no matter what powers Devin had. To make matters worse, the man in question was dead, thus there was no debate. It was an argument he couldn't win.

"Then why did he go to seek out Arianna Grace in order to marry her?" Devin asked in reply. The room quieted at his question.

"He never intended to marry Ms. Grace," Maureen replied, brushing off his question like it wasn't even a problem. "Even Nessa has admitted that much."

That was true. Nessa had stated that her brother didn't intend to marry Arianna, but Devin knew otherwise. Rhys grew desperate to win over Arianna, and tried to charm his way into her heart to no avail. By the end, Rhys caused a battle to grab his trophy with every intention of making her his. Devin looked to Fiona. Her eyes were downcast and she remained silent. She knew the truth as well. Devin was growing more certain that Rhys never had any intention of marrying Fiona once he met Arianna.

"And you?" Devin asked, pointing to Fiona. She still didn't look up at either Nessa or Devin. Fiona was the weak link. Rhys must have broken her heart.

"I support my mother on all she says," Fiona mumbled. The room was back to chaos. No one knew what to think of the news.

'I should have asked her yesterday,' Devin told Nessa.

Nessa faced him, and her anger increased. While he was getting used to it, Devin was a bit surprised. He had said the wrong thing again, though he wasn't quite sure what it was, exactly, that he said wrong.

'You knew?' Nessa asked, like he had set her up to be placed on the spot by Maureen. In fact, Devin was sure Fiona didn't want anyone to know. She had been nothing but scared and embarrassed when she saw him. It had to be all Maureen's doing.

'I ran into her yesterday. We didn't really talk. I just saw. She knew I saw and ran away,' Devin replied, trying to get Nessa to understand that it wasn't a big deal. Yet it obviously it was to her because she didn't calm down at Devin's explanation. He was in hot water again. Every time he thought he was winning her back over, he pissed her off. Nessa was a hard one to crack.

"The time for putting forth a new heir to the throne is done," Rolf told the crowd, trying to calm the noise of the chatter. "The council agreed a month ago that Nessa was the rightful heir and had set the date that was only three days away. Maureen sat on that council herself. From the looks of it, Maureen knew about Fiona, and could have voiced her opposition then. She didn't, and thus there's nothing to discuss now. Next person. Thomas Knots," Rolf stated, trying to contain the situation. He was moving on. He had to. What else could they do?

However, Devin felt that the crowd wasn't convinced, even if it was true. Fiona was known to be the companion of the late king. As big as she was now, she had to have gotten pregnant well before the king left for a month and was subsequently killed. This was a matter that had to be dealt with, but Devin needed time to think. Too much was building up at one time—Maureen's claim to the throne just adding to the list—but right now it was more important to find the person poisoning everyone else. Devin had to agree and let Rolf move on with the grievances for now.

"Devin," Nessa's cousin, Ronan, called out as he burst into the room. All faces turned to the young, dark-haired man.

"There's been another poisoning, but the person is still alive. They need you."

Devin nodded to Ronan as he stood. "Sorry. I'll be back as soon as I can," he told Nessa as he leaned over and kissed her cheek, setting up the barrier to keep her safe again.

Nessa was a ball of confusion as he ran away. She was still angry, but hopeful he could rescue the person that was dying. Devin grinned over the fact that her anger was simmering down as it had been full blast only moments before. He knew from the first time he met Nessa that she would be hard to keep track of, but it was all beginning to feel a bit more normal. He was getting used to the roller coaster of emotion from her, especially now that the bond was completely open. It was easier to see the world through her eyes and have more empathy for her. Now, he just wished she could do the same for him.

Devin followed behind Ronan as they left after healing the sidhe, leaving him awake and coherent. He had made it just in time to save the young man's life, even if the sidhe he was helping didn't appreciate being saved by a day human. The injured elite sidhe couldn't have been more than fifteen or sixteen years old, yet still disliked Devin extremely just for being a day human. No matter the young man's attitude, Devin hated to see someone so young caught in the war. The boy had a future ahead of him. Someone that age didn't have much time to be involved in any of the sidhe politics. He was probably innocent of any doings of his family or clan. Why would they poison such a young man for crimes he didn't commit? The elite needed to change.

He looked down at the new vial of poison he held. Though he didn't know what it was, it looked similar to what he had taken from all of the other places. He needed to find out what it was because he couldn't be there every time someone was poisoned. They required a solution that didn't involve calling in the day human that everyone despised. They had to stop the culprit, and stop the poison. Those were their two main goals. Everything else had to come in second.

"You know that the nobles would be forced to listen to you if you would just marry my cousin," Ronan told Devin as they slowed down once they rounded the corner to the amphitheater where Nessa had been left again. Devin wasn't anxious to see what he found there. She would be pissed.

Marriage had crossed his mind several times in the last two days. They had been bonded for months now, but they'd both thought it was temporary. Their lives were intertwined, and so were the emotions that pulled them together. Marriage seemed like the next best option, especially with Nessa becoming queen soon. Regardless, there was no way he was going to allow someone else to marry her. She meant too much to him. It filled him with jealousy just to see another gaze upon her in a desirable way.

"That would work if there was ever the time to ask her," Devin replied, which was the truth of it.

"So you don't have time to talk? What do you two do all day?" Ronan teased as they slowed.

Devin grinned at the insinuation. He would have liked that to be true, but their relationship was also lacking in that department. First, he needed to learn how to navigate the emotional nightmare that was Nessa. "You know your cousin. She's always mad about something. There hasn't been a time to ask her when she is in a good mood and has recently forgiven me for something I did."

Ronan laughed and patted Devin on the back. "That I can believe." Ronan pointed into the room where Nessa was still sitting, glaring at the doorway they had just entered.

Nessa was mad, fuming to be exact. She had been left alone in the empty amphitheater in Devin's protective bubble. She was safe from anyone harming her, but she also couldn't move, which could have been a problem if she needed anything

When Devin reached her, he offered her his hand, breaking the bubble. Nessa took it, but once she could move, threw his hand back down.

"What the heck was that?" Nessa asked, marching out of the room.

"I was just keeping you safe," Devin replied, following behind her.

"Safe? No. That was keeping me prisoner," she spat out as she made her way to her wing of the palace. "And isn't that what they're for?" Nessa pointed to the invisible sidhe assassins that Devin had assigned to follow Nessa all of the time. Two stayed beside her and two behind her. Nessa didn't like Devin in his protective mode. She wanted to protect herself.

Devin grinned. He had taught Nessa how to see through sidhe magic, and now she could do it without thinking. That was one of the things he loved about her. She might be a night human, and she might be a sidhe, but she was different in how she thought. None of the other sidhe could be taught to see behind the magic. They would never believe it was possible, let alone be able to do it. Nessa could.

Nessa stared at Devin in shock when he smiled at her anger. She stomped into her apartment, and he stopped beside Ronan to say good-bye to him. Devin knew grinning was the wrong reaction as soon as she slammed the door in his face. Ronan began to laugh.

"I understand your troubles, and I don't see a solution any time soon," Ronan replied. He patted Devin on the back. "Good luck with her. I'd like to blame her family, but that would implicate me."

At that, Devin shrugged and grinned at Ronan. He didn't see his life being different with Nessa, even if he tried. If he attempted to protect any other girl, they would melt at the gesture, but not Nessa. He knew, through the bond, that she did appreciate his effort to keep her safe, but she would never admit it out loud. She was too strong for that. Nessa was just one more puzzle he had to figure out, and he was running out of time. In two days Nessa would be crowned … if they could get everything under control. He'd have to move quicker if he wanted to stand beside her at her coronation. He wanted to let her know she wasn't alone, that he was never going to leave her lonely.

Devin stared at the closed door. When he saw the magic that lined the door, he knew she wasn't about to let him in. She was seriously mad. Grinning, Devin placed his hand on her magic, adding his own protection to the whole room. She was back in her protective bubble, but at least this time, it was large enough that he hoped she wouldn't notice. There was no use waiting around. Since she could be mad for hours, Devin turned from her apartment.

It was getting lighter as day approached, and Devin made his way outside the palace. Nessa would need to be asleep before he could go back in. He could break her spell with his new abilities, but he knew better than to try. She would still be mad from the protective spell he'd put on her earlier, and didn't need her pissed that he was able to break the spells that were meant to keep him out. He understood that she needed her privacy to sulk a bit.

Devin left through the unguarded doorway and ventured into the village. No one would even know he was gone. He had learned much more about the sidhe by sitting in on their complaints, but he still needed to see everything with his own eyes. His connection to the common sidhe grew with each moment he was in the village and around them. He could sympathize with them because he knew what it was like growing up in Lord Randolph's estate. Devin wasn't an elite dearg-dul, but he lived in that world and was always out of place. He was a lowly day human, just like the elite viewed the common sidhe as less than them. Many of the dearg-dul leaders despised him, but he could do nothing to change that. He was only a kid when he was taken in and quickly learned about the divisions that were all too prevalent in the night human world. The common sidhe had those same borders and were treated the same way that he was as a child, so he understood their world.

As Devin wandered around, people were locking up to go to bed. Most didn't even pay attention to him. A few did stop to stare as he passed, and a few more were people he had met earlier in the night. They didn't stop him, but they did look at him differently. Devin hated that feeling, but knew he had done the right thing. He'd helped Nessa out and helped the common sidhe out as well, since he could understand their world more than Nessa could. Life outside of the palace was more relaxed and definitely where Devin felt he belonged. Nessa could handle the elite and their selfish ways. He would be there for the common sidhe with their *real* problems.

It didn't take long for Devin to walk out of the level dirt path to another pathway outside of the main village. He continued to wander, and stopped to watch a younger female sidhe as she talked to the flowers in her garden. She piqued his interest immediately because she was the only person he'd found actually doing sidhe magic. The seedlings were small, yet growing as she talked. Soon the petals opened as she coaxed them. One by one, the flowers completely opened, her voice providing the motivation to grow. *How could she make a flower grow?* he wondered, watching intently. Once the last flower was completely grown and open, she wiped her hands and stood back up from her kneeling position. Devin was in awe; he had never seen anything like it, and couldn't have imagined it before actually seeing it. There was much he had to learn.

The young girl jumped when she finally lifted her eyes and saw Devin standing there, watching her. He held up his hands in surrender to try to calm the girl, watching as several emotions crossed her face: surprise, shyness, panic, and even curiosity. She was torn between running back inside of her house and looking at Devin. He smiled, hoping it would calm her. She reminded him of the deer he'd come across a deer in the forest. Her big brown eyes were eying him.

"I didn't mean to scare you," Devin said softly, trying his best to not make the young sidhe run away from him. "I just was watching. I've never seen someone do that before."

The girl blushed. "It's nothing," she said in a mere whisper, obviously not used to compliments.

"Nothing?" Devin replied. How could she think that? "You made the flower grow and open." It still amazed him to see that done. It wasn't an illusion. She had grown a real flower.

"Making flowers grow really isn't a useful power, my dad used to say," she replied. "He said if I could control my power and make trees grow, I'd have been marriageable." The girl shrugged, growing more confident in talking to Devin. He was glad. He wanted to know more and hated that everyone was wary of him.

"You can make trees grow?" Devin asked in surprise. That would be another power he had if he wanted to learn how to do it. The old king had given Devin the ability to do anything the sidhe could do. Devin was beginning to see that what he could do now was a bit boundless.

"Nah, that's why I ended up here," the girl replied, motioning around her. Devin had not noticed he was surrounded by crude, lean-to houses. From the cracks in the hastily-put-together homes, faces watched him. There wasn't order like there had been on the road, and now it was more of a messy camp than city. Devin finally realized he had walked exactly where the little girl had told him the day before. He was in the castoff's camp that he had wanted to visit.

"Because you couldn't grow trees?" Devin asked. That seemed like a strange reason to disown your child.

She shrugged. "Sort of," she replied, still eyeing him over. As if she suddenly remembered, her tone changed to urgent. "You really should get back to your owner. You will get in much more trouble if they find you here. No one is supposed to come to this side of town, especially not a day human. You shouldn't wander from your owner. Not everyone is nice enough to leave you alone."

Devin smiled at the idea that his owner wouldn't let him wander. Devin had no owner, but completely understood what the girl meant. Nessa was worried about Devin being in the sidhe village as day human were considered pets, but Devin wasn't worried, not before, and especially not now.

"I'm free to go as I please," Devin replied, not commenting on the owner part. It was best to keep his identity a secret.

"Mara," a male voiced called as he came through the woods and into view. "I found another seed. I'd like to see how it grows." The young man came into the garden and wrapped the woman in a gigantic hug.

Mara squealed a little and nodded toward Devin. The male sidhe stopped and stared at him with the same deer-eyed look, unsure if he should run or talk. Devin didn't mind being a curiosity as long as it meant they weren't running in fear.

"Hi," Devin said, breaking the ice. "I was just walking around and saw ..." Devin didn't know what to call the girl.

"My wife, Mara," the man replied proudly.

The man set the girl down and wiped his face with the rag on his belt. With some of the dirt gone, Devin could see that he was just as young as the girl. Devin had to guess they might only be teenagers, or in their early twenties at most. Why were they alone in the castoff's village and married?

"I just was passing by when I saw her growing a flower," Devin explained. "I have never seen that before."

The young man grinned. "That's my Mara. She has quite a unique ability," he replied proudly. "Not everyone can use just words to get a flower to grow."

"I'd say," Devin answered. All of the sidhe were amazing to him, but the young man was confirming that Mara was even more unique.

"And what would a day human be doing out without their master? I assure you that we are safe, but I still don't think you should be here. When whoever owns you comes back, they will be upset to find you here. The elite aren't really fans of the common sidhe, let alone us," he told Devin, pointing around the camp.

"I have no owner," Devin replied for a second time. "I came here on my own, and won't be in trouble."

The young man looked dubiously at Devin. All day humans had an owner in the sidhe world. Devin could understand the confusion, but there was no way to say it any clearer without telling them who he really was, and he wasn't about to do that.

"I assure you. I really have no owner," Devin added in the face of their disbelief. The young man still didn't look convinced, but shook his head like he'd humor Devin. "Actually, yesterday I met a little girl that told me about this place. I wandered here by accident, or maybe fate."

That answer seemed more to the liking of the castoff sidhe. He couldn't understand Devin being free, but he could understand wandering off. Devin had to suppress a grin. The sidhe were funny people.

"How long have you been in the village?" the young man asked.

Devin shrugged. "Only a few days." Devin was slowly losing count of how long he had been in the sidhe village. Had it only been days? It felt much longer to him.

"Then you still have a lot to see," the man replied.

Devin nodded. He did have a lot to see, but this was enough to make him sad. The dirty faces that watched him from the dark corners were not bad people; he could feel the good all around him. They were normal sidhe who didn't fit in with the plans of the elite, and had been thrown away, as the little girl had told him, for things such as love.

"How did you two end up here?" Devin asked, still looking around at the hiding faces. Some were old, but many were young.

The young man chuckled. "You sure are curious for a day human." Mara nodded. Devin was unsure how to take that. He doubted they had met many day humans.

"This place is different from where I'm used to," Devin replied. He was curious. He needed to be. How was he to save the sidhe if he didn't understand them?

Smiling, the young man nodded. "Fair enough. I'm sure I'd find where you are from different, too." The young man draped an arm around Mara. "I grew up in town, basically on the other side of town from here. I was part of the Miller family, and Mara was a Ferguson. We used to see each other during our chores, and discovered our abilities are similar. While she can grow plants, I can make fruit and seeds grow on trees. We crossed paths often and became friends. When her father went to publicly disown her for not being able to grow more than flowers, I found out I loved her. So we decided to be together. Since I had claimed her, her family and father actually agreed to let her marry me. Her father was just afraid he would never have her married. Once we were, he didn't find anything wrong with her ability. I don't know how much of the politics you have been told, but you don't mix families. Eventually word got to the heads of the families, and the Millers and Fergusons disowned us. We ended up here. Not the best way to start a marriage, but it has worked for us."

"I'd have ended up here anyway," Mara added, "but this lug thought he was being all chivalrous by calling out that he loved me. He thought if I was disowned I could join his family. That was not the case when the elite found out."

"And so you have to live here?" Devin asked. It was on the outskirts of the village and run down, but he didn't see why it was bad off. They were free of the elite.

"Yes, and we are not allow to participate in functions of the village," Mara added. She shrugged. "It's not too bad. We've had to learn how to become self-sufficient, but everyone around here helps you learn."

The young man raised his eyebrows. "Not too bad?"

Mara tried to shush him. "Colin, not now."

Colin turned to Devin. "Enjoy your life with the elite sidhe, because with them, even as a slave, you still will have more than we do. We are not allowed to participate is the nice way of saying we are cut off. While the village works with cooperation from everyone together, we are not part of the everyone." Mara looked shocked at his words. It was obvious Colin was hitting on a subject not spoken out loud.

"What do you mean part of *the everyone*?" Devin asked. Colin was passionate, and Devin was sure he would answer, even with Mara's panicked look. Devin kind of liked Colin. He wasn't beating around the bush or lying. Maybe he wasn't supposed to say what he had, but Devin needed to hear the truth.

"I don't know how much you've seen or been told, but the way the village works is that each person has a job. We work together to survive. The butcher provides meat to all while the baker provides bread. Either your ability gives you a position to help the community, or you apprentice at a job that's the best fit. We work together to survive. When you live out here, there is nothing. You no longer get meat from the butcher. You can't apprentice. We have to survive on the skills we have, and trust me, fruit as a diet got old two days after moving here."

Mara was still looking around like some unknown, invisible sidhe would hear his words. Devin had the feeling that the castoffs were not allowed to complain. Why would it matter? They were already outcasts from society.

"So how do you survive?" Devin asked quietly. It was obvious that the conversation was making Mara worry.

"If we are lucky, we can sell our abilities to the elite sidhe. Good thing they like their fruit ripened just perfect," Colin replied.

"So they pay you for it?" Devin asked. The sidhe didn't seem like a money society.

"They give us supplies in return for maybe a quarter of the value of our services," Colin replied. They were cheated by the elite. Not a surprise.

"That doesn't seem fair," Devin said.

"Fair? The elite don't know what fair even means," Colin huffed. Mara quickly covered his mouth.

"Hush now. No more talk of this," Mara scolded both Colin and Devin. "If they hear you complaining, they won't take your fruit."

Devin nodded. He didn't want his questions to keep Mara and Colin from getting the supplies they needed. Colin didn't look like he had said enough, but with Mara's begging, he stopped. Their life was harder than Devin expected, and it was due to the elite having unnecessary rules. Why couldn't someone from one family marry another? What was the harm in that? Where was the harm in love?

Devin looked around the camp one more time. He could feel the anxiety of the people around him. They either feared what Colin had said, or they feared Devin. Maybe they thought Devin would go tell the elite. He had no way to calm them. He knew that as much as he wanted to see more, he was sure that he needed to let the people be for now. There would always be more time to learn about the castoffs, especially when they were not as anxious.

Devin wandered back to the palace and hoped to find Nessa sleeping. He needed a bit of rest too as the morning sun rose. It wasn't normal that Devin craved sleep, but he felt it now. Devin stopped as he turned at the end of the hallway leading to Nessa's quarters. She stood in the doorway with her hands on her hips. She wasn't asleep after all, and she wasn't happy to see him.

CHAPTER 5

Devin was surprised that Nessa actually let him back into the room, but he wasn't about to mention it to her. He already knew—from peeking in her mind—that she'd been mad at him for maybe five minutes after he had left, and then released her magic to let him in. He wasn't there waiting as she expected, and when she couldn't leave the room to find him, she became angry again. He was forgiven for a moment, but was not there for it. Now she was back to being mad. Devin couldn't help but smile. He had a feeling his whole life with Nessa would be like that.

Nessa ignored Devin as she'd gotten ready for bed. Even though she went to sleep without a single word to him, she'd forgiven him enough to let him sleep in the bed beside her and not on the couch.

Devin listened as Nessa slept peacefully. It turned out that she wasn't comfortable with having him gone after all. Watching her sleep, he couldn't help but think that she had no idea how beautiful she was with her dark curls. He reached forward and wrapped one around his finger.

She had been very sheltered from the sidhe life. He was sure that she knew nothing of the castoffs, or even much about the common sidhe in general. It would break her heart to know that there was a whole part of her village that lived on the bare essentials. She had too much compassion to let it stay as it was, but he didn't want to witness how much it would hurt her when she eventually found out. Devin needed to change the life for the common sidhe and the castoffs to something Nessa could live with.

Slowly, Devin leaned forward and kissed her forehead. He hadn't slept much, maybe a few hours before he had woken again, but he wanted to go back out into the village. It would be early for the sidhe, but fine for him. He needed to find a way to help the castoffs.

Nessa's eyes cracked open when the bed shifted. "Where are you going now?"

"Just for a run," Devin replied, which was kind of true.

Nessa nodded as she closed her eyes again. She wasn't mad at him any longer, or at least she didn't stay mad while sleeping. Smiling, Devin stood up. He going to have to ask her to marry him soon, as there was no way he could take any of the other sidhe who were coming to the village coronation eyeing her over. That might just be enough to make him loose his cool. She would be his with all of the ups and downs that followed.

"Come back soon," Nessa said sleepily as Devin opened the door to their bedroom.

"Always," Devin replied. He could never leave her for long.

Devin made his way back out of the palace and into the streets. He'd intended to go talk to the castoffs again, but when he saw Old Man Winters pulling his cart in the fading sunlight—which most night humans avoided—Devin hurried over to the old man and took the cart from him.

"Young day human." The old man chuckled. "Is rescuing an old man your new pastime?"

"Horse still not well?" Devin asked in reply. He did want to see the castoffs, but he needed to help the older man first.

"I think she is better, but I'm giving her one more day off," the man replied with a shrug, as if pulling a cart full of milk wasn't a problem for his old body.

Devin nodded, strolling alongside the older man. This time, as they moved through the town, they stopped at the houses on the other side of the street. Devin waited each time as the old man limped over and took the pitcher from the resident. Less people stared at Devin and more just went on with their lives. He had been an oddity his first time through the village, but now he was not and for that he was thankful.

As they reached the last house, and Devin helped Old Man Winters pull the empty jugs of milk back toward the barn, Devin realized that there were still two jugs filled with milk. He was sure that they were done, but there was milk left.

"Do you always have this much left?" Devin asked. He didn't see any homes that they had missed.

"Sometimes," Winters replied as he shooed two cows away from the door to the barn.

"What do you do with it?" Devin asked. It wasn't like they had refrigerated storage in their natural world.

"We try to use what we can, but mostly we give back to the animals around the farm. The cows are doing very well right now, and I've had more than enough to feed everyone in town for months," he replied. When he pulled on the door, the cows finally moved. The old man hobbled over to the tanks of milk and took them down.

"Would I be able to take some to others that need it?" Devin asked.

"As in others that are not visited?" the older man asked with a wink. He knew immediately what Devin planned to do with the milk.

"I don't want to get you in trouble," Devin replied. Devin was unsure about the laws and what would be enough to get one thrown in with the castoffs, but truly didn't want to cause waves for the old man. Plus, he wasn't *actually* asking the old man to help him.

The old man held up a hand to keep Devin from talking more.

"If you'd like to borrow a cart, and maybe find another use for that milk, I'm heading inside for a quick nap before I get to my chores. I'll have no clue what you are up to." He grinned at Devin, giving him the distinct feeling the old man knew exactly what he wanted to do, and was giving himself plausible deniability. "Not all of us think there should be people who are just thrown away. That isn't our way, it is the elite way. We are not elite, yet somehow they feel like they have the right to impose their rules on us. I wish I could help all that live here, but that's too risky. Without me, there would be no one to tend the farm. I have no family of my own, and have never been assigned an apprentice. When I die, so does my farm."

Devin nodded, and waved to the old man as he walked back into his home. He waited a moment—to make sure that the old man was completely uninvolved in what he was about to do—and then he put the milk back to the cart. He wasn't going to stand by and shun the castoffs for being who they were. Devin saw nothing wrong in them.

Pulling the milk cart through town, Devin noted that it was strange to see the people waking and starting their day. His other two walks were at dawn when the night humans were heading off to bed. Now it was dusk and the world was coming to life. Old Man Winters wasn't the only one out doing chores and delivering food. Devin watched as several other carts joined him on the road. They were all going about their day. No one seemed to even pay attention to him while they went about their tasks. For the first time in a long time, Devin felt like he fit in again … even though this was a night human world. This was a life he could live. The sidhe were different than where he was brought up. They seemed even more normal than the dearg-dul that Devin was raised beside. This was truly becoming his home now, he fit in here.

Devin made it to the edge of the village and the castoff area before anyone even looked at him. A few curious sidhe on the border stared, but none stopped him as he left the village for the overgrown pathway that was the castoff road. Pulling the cart got harder, but he managed to get it to the castoff camp without too much difficulty. Devin stopped first at Mara and Colin's house. Colin was outside with Mara, kissing her good-bye for the day.

"Day human, you couldn't stay away?" Colin called to Devin.

Devin balanced his cart. "I decided to take a walk and found some leftover milk. I thought everyone around here could use some."

Mara looked shocked, but Colin grinned. Devin could already tell he was winning Colin over. Mara still seemed to be caught in the sidhe world rules. It was a good thing she had Colin to keep her alive and learning how to do things without the other sidhe.

"The Maise and Connor families both have young children. I'm sure they could use some milk," Colin replied, pointing further into the makeshift town.

"Well, there is quite a lot left. How many people live here?" Devin asked. He hadn't thought before how much it would take to feed everyone, just that even one person was better to feed than none.

"Right now we are at eighty-two, twenty-five families," Mara whispered. She didn't seem as okay with the idea, even if she looked like she secretly wanted it. Devin was unsure what they even had to eat in the camp, but it was pretty clear that milk was a rarity.

Devin glanced back at the two jugs of milk that were almost full. He had watched Old Man Winters deliver milk to all of the sidhe in town. It wasn't hard to calculate. There was more than enough for twenty-five families.

"I'll start with the houses on the right, and make my way back around. There should be enough for everyone," Devin replied.

"You really shouldn't," Mara said, finding her voice a little more. "You'll get in trouble. No one is supposed to share with us. It's against the rules."

"Good thing I'm no one, then," Devin replied, trying to reassure the young sidhe woman.

He knew where her fear came from, but in reality, who was going to tell Devin no? While he understood order and rules, he also understood that the clans were just being vindictive toward these people. He didn't need to follow the rules if they were ridiculous. Colin nodded to Devin as he made his way down the uneven pathway.

Devin stopped at the first hovel. It wasn't much more than a few branches leaned against a tree with long grass hastily thrown upon it. It wouldn't keep out much of the weather, and Devin was sure it leaked in the rain. Two young faces peered out from the cracks of the branch walls.

"Ma'am," Devin called to the woman working the garden outside the home. The castoffs seemed to all have a garden to tend, which was probably their main food source. "I brought some milk."

The sidhe looked startled that she was being spoken to. She was even more shocked when she stood and noticed that Devin wasn't a sidhe. After deciding he was safe, she wiped her hands on her dress and cautiously approached him.

"Sidhe of the village are not allowed to share," she told

Devin. She obviously had the same fear as Mara.

"Then it's a good thing I'm not a sidhe," Devin replied. He smiled, and saw that would be enough to win her over. Being a day human in that moment was probably the best cover. He could plead ignorance, and the rules technically didn't apply to him since he wasn't one of them.

The lady hurried inside and returned with two large glasses. She didn't have a covered pitcher like the women in town. Devin had to wonder if the cups were the only ones she even had. His short glimpse in the house showed she had close to nothing. Devin ladled milk into the two cups. It would have to do, and it was better than nothing. He gave one last look to the children that were now watching the milk in their mother's hands.

"I'll pray that you don't get in trouble with your master," the woman said, bowing to Devin before going back into the house.

Devin made his way around to the other houses. It was much the same. The people were shocked at his offer, but no one declined. They were all desperate. Devin looked at each face and knew these were exactly the people the old sidhe king told him he needed to save. There were women, children, old, and young. They were sidhe, yet not allowed to be part of the town. By the time he made it back to the start, Mara was no longer outside. Devin walked through her beautiful garden filled with flowering plants of every color. Even her house was covered with plants that crawled up the sides and onto the roof. She opened the door as he made it closer.

"Do you have a pitcher I can fill?" he asked.

She looked like she wanted to say no, but her eyes were already watching the pails on the cart. He could not have guessed how long it had been since she had had milk. Leaving the door open, she went in and grabbed a small pitcher from the only shelf in the room. There was a blanket on the floor, which had to be their bed, and a short table in the one room. It wasn't much, but it seemed tidy and clean. Even without the normal sidhe world, Mara was still making a life. Devin filled her pitcher with milk and returned.

"They will punish you for this," she told him quietly. The lively girl that was singing to her flowers earlier was gone, replaced by the quiet women before him now. There was pain behind her eyes as if she knew exactly what lay in store for Devin. He longed to tell her who he was and make it all better, but he wanted to stay the welcomed day human, not the unwelcome day human prince.

"I will be fine," he tried to assure her, hoping it would be enough.

"No matter if you're right about not breaking any rules, your master will be upset," Mara replied. She was trying her best to get Devin to understand the sidhe world.

"I have no master," Devin told her for a second time. She still couldn't believe him. At least this time it seemed she had heard him and was considering the option. The young woman looked shocked at his words. In the sidhe world it was not possible to be a day human and not have a master. "Trust me. No one will be punished for this."

"But ..." Mara started and stopped. She was having a hard time, but was listening to Devin's words.

"I assure you, I will be fine," Devin told her. "As long as I head back soon and not upset my ..." Devin was unsure what to call Nessa.

Mara blushed as she understood. "You are here because of a girl?"

"Oh, yes. I'm not here to visit the sidhe, that's for sure. This was never on my list of destinations that I wanted to see," Devin replied, making his way back through the garden. He was trying to keep her thoughts on a brighter subject than him being punished, since he wouldn't be.

"And she is a sidhe?" Mara asked curiously.

"That she is," Devin replied, locking the lids back on the canisters.

"But she doesn't own you?" Mara asked, full of questions.

"No."

"Because she loves you," Mara added, finally understanding Devin a bit more.

Devin smiled and nodded. "I sure hope so. It would make asking her to marry me easier."

Mara's mouth hung open. "You plan to marry her? Sidhe only marry sidhe." She sounded like she was reading a textbook answer.

Devin grinned. "That may be, but as I said, I am special. I don't think anyone here has the power to tell us no if she does want to marry me."

Mara didn't seem to be able to believe that. She continued to stare at him, waiting for the joke that should have been coming, but Devin was serious. In that moment, he felt bad for not telling her, as he could have eased her worry.

"I'll try to come back in another day or so," Devin told Mara, making his way to the cart. "I'm sure there will be more milk that I can bring. Seems there has been an overabundance of milk lately, and it's just enough to feed you guys."

Mara did not respond. Apparently he had already done enough to shock her for one day.

As he made his way back through the village, the streets were flooded with sidhe; some of the people scurried from one place to another while others leisurely strolled. Old and young alike were out for the night. Children played and women sat around watching the children while they gossiped. Life continued on in the village, no matter what drama was in the elite homes and palace. Devin wanted to stop and watch it all, but he had to return the cart back and get to Nessa soon, as she had to be awake by now. When he made it to the end of the dirt path and Old Man Winters's farm, Devin dropped the cart and rushed forward. Two sidhe palace guards were dragging the old man from his house.

"What's going on?" Devin demanded to know. He stood in the open gate to the house to stop them from going further.

"Out of the way, day human." One guard tried to push Devin from blocking the walkway.

"Young day human, be on your way," Winters told Devin, siding with the guards. "This is none of your business."

Devin didn't move from his spot. "I demand to know what's going on." Devin glared at each man, daring them to try to move him. The two sidhe exchanged a look. They were surprised, and slightly amused, at Devin's audacity.

"Day humans have no business in the affairs of the sidhe. Now move before we have to take you back with us," the shorter of the two guards told Devin. They were no match for him before he got his power, and stood no chance now. Devin was not moving.

"Under whose authority are you acting?" Devin demanded to know.

The taller sidhe looked to the shorter. They obviously didn't want to harm Devin, as they didn't know which family he belonged to, but Devin was stopping them from their orders. They would need to make a choice and soon to get the old man back to the palace like they had been ordered.

"Lady Maureen asked us to arrest this man. He has been found to be aiding the castoff sidhe, and that's against the law," the shorter man replied. Devin didn't move.

"Well, you two may go back and tell Lady Maureen that she has no authority over what I have told this man he can do,"

Devin replied.

The two men laughed and moved to push Devin out of the way. Devin held his ground as the two swords of the late king appeared on his back. If he had to fight the men, he would. Maureen was the last person Devin was going to allow to bully the common sidhe. He already disliked the lady with a passion for her attempts to kill Nessa through her children, and she was not earning any more points for her actions with the common sidhe.

Both guards immediately dropped the arms of the older man when they saw the swords, fell to their knees, and bowed their heads. Now they knew who he was.

"Please forgive us, Day Human Prince." The taller man spoke, as it seemed the shorter man was now at a loss for words.

"As I said before, I can do as I please. This man had nothing to do with aiding the castoffs. It was completely my doing. Please go back and inform Lady Maureen that she shouldn't hastily prosecute people when she doesn't know the full story. I might not be in as good a mood next time," Devin warned the two men. They stood and nodded before quickly retreating into the village. Devin would have never responded with violence against the two guards that were only doing their jobs, but he was threatening enough that they didn't know the difference.

Devin went over to help the older man stand since they'd dropped him at the sight of Devin's swords. He grinned as Devin pulled him up.

"I think I understand now why you have no fear of us," the old man said, dusting off his pants. "Because in reality we should all fear you, Day Human Prince."

"I don't wish to be feared by the common sidhe, just the elite," Devin replied. It made life in the palace tolerable when they didn't treat him like trash. It made doing as he pleased much easier.

The old man smiled. "Then your secret is safe with me."

Nessa paced around her room some more. Devin had not returned yet. He was outside of the palace walls, but she had no clue what he was doing. He had said he was going for a run, which could have been the case, but she guessed that he had different plans. The common sidhe seemed to fascinate him, but there wasn't any real reason for that. They were just sidhe like everyone else, with a little less power than the elite sidhe. What was interesting about them?

Nessa didn't need to check to know that Devin had placed his magic around the room to keep her in. It would be a waste of energy to try to get out at this point. She wanted to be mad at him for it, but she couldn't. He was doing his best to protect her. Not that she wanted to admit it, but she did need help being protected. Between assassins and poison, in less than a week, there had been several attempts on her life. He was the only reason she was still alive … but it still hurt nonetheless. Nessa wanted to be able to protect herself, and letting Devin do it for her went against every idea she was raised on.

Nessa turned around the room one more time before she went to her door and opened it. Since there was a protective bubble around the room, she didn't need to worry about anyone entering without her knowledge. Therefore, she could leave the door wide open to watch for Devin. Nessa made another loop around the room and neared the doorway again.

'*Where are you?*' Nessa finally asked Devin silently. She was doing her best to not beg him to come back, but her self-control failed. She wanted to know what he was up to.

'*Just inside of the courtyard. I'll be back in less than a minute,*' Devin replied. He laughed a little in Nessa's head, and he had to know how much she wanted out of the cage he had put her in.

Down the hallway, Ronan and Gemma were walking toward Nessa's rooms. Nessa waved to her cousins. It was nice that they would come keep her company in her protective bubble. Gemma paused and rubbed her neck before she began to lightly run in her direction. Nessa never knew where Gemma got all of her energy from. Ronan shook his head and kept his leisurely pace as he walked behind her. Soon Devin caught up to Ronan and said something to her cousin to make him laugh. Nessa wanted out of her cage, to be able to walk with them, but she waited as patiently as she could for them to get to her.

'Move now,' Devin told Nessa mentally, with more urgency than she had ever heard him use. Nessa scrambled out of the doorway and back into the room as Gemma hit the barrier of the spell and fell forward.

"What—" Nessa began to ask as Devin and Ronan ran in behind her cousin.

Devin took Gemma and pulled her completely inside of the room while Ronan looked behind them before closing the door.

"Someone just attacked Gemma and Ronan," Devin told Nessa. He was in full alert mode. Even though he wanted to go after the assassin who had to be close, he was concerned for her cousins first and foremost.

She glanced between her cousins, who didn't appear hurt. She had been standing right there watching. No one had attacked anyone, unless they were invisible. Where the assassin? No one could do an invisibility spell now because of Devin, but it made no sense. How did Devin know they were attacked and how did it happen? It was confusing, but Nessa trusted that Devin knew what was going on.

Devin rolled Gemma to her side and pulled a small dart out of her neck. It was smaller than a fly, but there was no mistaking what it was. Someone had attacked Gemma with a dart. Ronan flopped down on the couch and dropped his own dart next to Gemma's on the table. He was still awake, but seemed to be fading fast. On the other hand, Gemma was already passed out. Nessa stared down to her younger cousin. It made no sense. Why would someone attack Gemma? She was the sweetest and most innocent person in their family.

Devin looked up to Nessa. "I think they were poisoned again. I can feel it inside of Gemma."

Nessa turned to Ronan. If Gemma was poisoned, then so was he. Nessa became increasingly worried as she glanced between them. They were the last of her family; her father had only one brother, and he only had two children. Gemma and Ronan were it, and Nessa was about to lose them, too. *Why was her life like this?* She wanted to be normal and not worry about people dying. However, there was no time for a pity party; Gemma and Ronan were poisoned and would die if they didn't act fast.

"Go find my uncle," Nessa instructed one of the invisible guards that were standing in the corners of the room. He needed to be there for his children. The guard nodded and exited the room without opening the door.

Devin moved to Ronan and inspected him quickly, too. Nessa watched, hoping Devin knew exactly what to do as he had before with her.

"You've both been poisoned," Devin told Ronan as Nessa expected.

"Take care of her first," Ronan replied, pointing to his unconscious sister. "She obviously got more in her system. At least I am still with you here." Ronan tapped his head before leaning back on to the couch. How long he would be with them was up for debate since the poison was also racing through his system.

Nessa knelt beside her younger cousin. Gently, she cupped her face in her hands; Gemma looked like she was sleeping. This was a quick-acting poison, and had to be something different than before. Did that mean there were more assassins running around now?

"Gems," Nessa said quietly, tapping her face gently. Unfortunately, Gemma didn't respond. Nessa wanted her to wake and pretend like it was a game and everything was fine … but it wasn't. Gemma was dying.

"Lay her on her back," Devin instructed.

Nessa rolled Gemma over, and when he placed his hands on her, Nessa felt the magic grow. How could Gemma get that sick in seconds? It took Nessa more than ten minutes before the poison took over. Nessa held on to her cousin's head, not watching as Devin cut her younger cousin. Devin began to pull the poison from her, and it couldn't have been pleasant for Gemma with how hard he was working. Gemma was one of the most innocent sidhe out there. She'd never been trained in combat, like Nessa had been, and she'd been kept away from all of the politics. Gemma was all that was sweet in the sidhe world. It made no sense. Why would someone target her?

Devin placed the poison into an empty vial that was sitting on the table. He had been collecting the poisons, but Nessa had no clue why … nor did she care at that point. He was able to save Gemma and she would live, which was what mattered the most.

"Ronan," Devin said, bringing Nessa's attention back to her older cousin, "how are you doing?"

"Better than she was," Ronan replied. He was now lying down on the couch.

At that moment, Rolf burst through the doorway with

Nessa's invisible guard.

"What happened?" he demanded, looking between his unconscious daughter and dying son. Rolf ran to Ronan's side and reached for his hand.

However, Nessa jumped up and stopped her uncle from touching Ronan. Devin was already working on trying to get the poison out of him, and Nessa didn't want him to stop. She needed her older cousin saved as well.

"I'm not sure," Nessa told her uncle, pulling him back a few steps. "They were walking this way, and suddenly Gemma collapsed. Devin found those darts on each of them. It appears someone poisoned them. Devin already got it out of Gemma, but he is still working on Ronan."

Rolf calmed down a little bit as he knelt at his son's side. There was nothing the older sidhe could do. There was nothing Nessa could do. They had to depend on Devin and hope that he could get it out in time.

Devin concentrated on the poison. This time, Nessa watched as Devin made a small cut just near Ronan's ribcage. Devin tugged and the poison began to leave Ronan's body. However, as Devin pulled on the string of poison, it suddenly snapped and went back into Ronan's body through the still-open cut.

"What was that?" Nessa asked. She had seen Devin remove poison from several people already, and that had never happened. This was different.

"I don't know," Devin replied as he began to remove the poison again. Less came out this time, and again it snapped back into Ronan. Devin stared at Ronan like he was a mystery. The poison felt the same but was acting differently.

"But you can't just leave it in him," Nessa argued as Ronan began to close his eyes, either from the poison or the pain.

"Why doesn't it come out?" Devin asked Rolf. He'd had no

training in sidhe poisons and was just doing what came naturally. Rolf was the only one that they could turn to, as Nessa didn't know much about sidhe poisons, either.

"It came out of Gemma?" Rolf asked, taking his son's hand the moment Devin wasn't working.

"Yes," Nessa replied. It didn't make any sense at all. The darts looked the same, the poison was the same amber color … everything seemed the same. Why did it come out of one and not the other? Were there two assassins?

Rolf stared at his son, thinking. He had a lot of knowledge in his years beside his brother and nephew when they were kings. This was completely Rolf's world, in every sense of the word, and he needed to search his mind for an answer. His son's life depended on it. Suddenly, his face fell when he realized the answer.

"It's clauthau poison," Rolf finally told them.

"Which is?" Devin prompted. Talking would get them nowhere unless he could do something to save Ronan.

"An ancient poison I didn't even know existed anymore," Rolf replied. "Once it enters the body, it gets a hold of you and can't be pulled out using the rare magic you possess."

"Then what do we do?" Nessa asked. Ronan's life was on the line. She turned to Devin, pleading with her eyes to save Ronan.

Devin glanced back down at Ronan. *What could they do with a poison that couldn't be removed?* Nessa watched Devin circle the poison through Ronan again. He could move it, just couldn't move it out of his body.

"Nessa, remove his shoes," Devin instructed her, and Nessa immediately did as he'd asked. She had no clue what Devin wanted to do, but she trusted him … she always trusted him.

Rolf looked at Devin. He had begun saying his good-byes to his son, but stopped when Nessa took off Ronan's shoes.

"What are you doing?" Rolf asked as Devin's magic heated up, causing the poison to once again move through Ronan's body.

"Hold him down," Devin told the older man. Rolf hesitated, and Devin stared at him. "Do you want your son to live?" This time there was no hesitation as he pinned his son's upper body down.

"Heat the sharpest blade we have in the fire," Devin told Nessa.

She ran over to the weapons and did exactly as he'd asked, watching Devin as she stood by the fire waiting for his next command. The blade in her hand was already red in color. Devin had worked the poison through Ronan's body and he writhed in pain, but Rolf continued to hold him down. They would do anything to save Ronan, and Nessa and her uncle hoped that Devin could do a miracle.

"I may not be able to pull the poison out," Devin finally explained, "but I can still move it. All of the poison is in his last two toes."

Rolf stared at Devin, understanding what he meant. Nessa understood also as she held the hot blade. Devin was going to remove the poison by removing Ronan's toes. It was a small sacrifice to pay to stay alive. Rolf wouldn't object, and neither would Ronan if he were still awake. Nessa had no clue how Devin came up with the plan, but she was sure it was the right thing to do.

"I'm not sure this will work, but I hope it will. Do I have permission to do it?" Devin asked Rolf.

Nessa was shocked. She had never seen him ask permission before. Devin always did what he thought was right... and he obviously thought it was right to remove Ronan's toes in order to save his life. However, Devin wasn't from the sidhe world, and was just working with what knowledge he had.

"Yes, do it before it spreads," Rolf replied, placing his full weight on Ronan's upper body. It was going to hurt terribly.

Devin held out his hand, and Nessa brought him the knife. She didn't want to watch, but she had to. She had to see if this could save Ronan's life no matter how much pain it would cause him. Devin didn't hesitate with the hot blade and cut down into the flesh at the top of Ronan's toes. Still not awake, Ronan screamed in his sleeping state. The smell of burned flesh was overwhelming.

"Heat it again," Devin directed Nessa, handing her back the blade. She hurried over and made the blade glow once more.

Devin pressed the blade to the still seeping foot. Nessa heard the sizzle and had to look away. Ronan didn't scream this time because he had completely passed out. Devin took the bandage one of Nessa's guards had brought, and gently wrapped up the foot. There was nothing more that they could do. If Devin's guess was correct, the poison would be in the detached toes and Ronan would be safe.

"Is it ..." Rolf finally asked as Devin stood up.

"All right?" Devin added to the question, and quickly searched Ronan's body. "Yes, the poison is in the toes I cut off. He is poison-free now. Ronan will be fine."

CHAPTER 6

After Ronan was attacked, Nessa insisted that Ronan and Gemma stay in her protected wing of the palace. Devin couldn't disagree. He had put both of them to sleep after he'd saved their lives, and they would be out of it for at least another day. Too much had happened too quickly. Devin needed time to sort out everything. Someone was still on the loose attacking people. He needed to find out who it was and soon. More sidhe would be arriving the next day for Nessa's coronation, and he couldn't risk an assassin causing war between the sidhe villages, let alone allow Nessa to stand in front as a big bullseye to whoever was trying to kill off everyone.

"You can't just leave us," Nessa complained after Devin had told her that he was going away again. She had followed him to the courtyard where he paused.

"I need to know what this is," Devin said, pointing to the vials of poison he carried. "I need to know if there is an antidote, and what it's made of. Rolf was sure no one had access to it when it was destroyed over five decades ago, but he doesn't even know what it was. He said it was a poison people spoke of but very few knew how to make it, and obviously someone kept the secret alive. We need to know what clauthau is and where to look for it. That just might be the clue we need to find out who's doing this."

"I get that, but you can't leave us here," Nessa complained.

Devin understood what she was saying. It wasn't that he was leaving that was the problem; it was that he was leaving her behind. He didn't want to, and he would have taken her with him in an instant, but she needed to stay and take care of the sidhe.

"Nessa," Devin took her hands in his, "I'd take you with in a heartbeat, but you have to remain here. Someone has to stay to make the decisions."

"But you said you'd only be gone for fifteen minutes." She pouted. Yes, she wanted to go with him. Maybe she wasn't as disgusted by the outside world as she pretended.

"And if something comes up in those fifteen minutes? You need to stay here to tell people what to do," Devin replied as gently as he could.

"Let Rolf take care of it," Nessa replied. She really wanted to go with him.

Devin shook his head. Normally Rolf would be a good person to leave in charge, but he was completely useless at this point. He was still too worried over his children. Devin couldn't ask him to step away and be a leader at that point. He needed to be a father until his children woke up feeling okay again.

"Fine, he can't take care of anything right now," Nessa admitted. She, too, saw her uncle was devastated by the poisoning of his children. "But what if something really comes up? What if someone else is poisoned? I can't do anything about it. You should stay and let me go."

Devin smiled. She wasn't making it easy. More than anything he wanted to scoop her into his arms and take her everyplace with him. He didn't feel safe leaving her alone, especially not now that the assassin had switched poisons, but he needed to get the samples to Mori to analyze. The computer tech and lab scientist at the dearg-dul estate Devin was raised at would be able to tell Devin exactly what the poison was, and that was crucial information they needed now.

Before setting off, Devin pulled Nessa close and hugged her tightly. *It would only be a few minutes and she would be fine.* Logically he knew that, but his heart didn't want to listen. It was hard to deal with his new feelings. Logic had always won easily, but now it wasn't that easy to walk away from her.

"I'll do everything in my power be back quickly. I can't stand to be away from you, so please stop worrying. I have to do this, and I'll be back soon. I'm not running away, I promise. I need to keep you safe, and this is me keeping you safe," Devin explained. Nessa melted in his arms. He could feel some of the fear run off of her.

"It's just that—" Nessa began to protest.

Devin put his lips to hers, abruptly ending her sentence. Her complaining stopped and her arms moved around him to hold on to his back. Her lips moved against his, too. She needed this kiss as much as Devin did. As he pulled back all too soon, the pout returned to Nessa's lips. Smiling, Devin quickly kissed her once more. She didn't like what he was doing, but she understood what needed to be done.

"I promise to be back soon," he told her.

"But," Nessa finally went to complain again, "you can't leave from here. Just let me go with you, I can help you." Devin loved her tenacity.

Devin planned to travel using the trees as Nessa had shown him once. He had no clue how to actually do it, but he was sure—like everything else—it would come naturally to him. Spotting the tree he was looking for, he took Nessa's hand and walked her to the bench beside it, sitting her down.

"I'll go to Mori and be back as soon as I can. I *promise* to come back," Devin repeated to her once again, and gently kissed her forehead. Instantly the bubble formed around her, just as he knew it would.

Hurrying to the tree, he placed his hand against it. Out of the corner of his eye, he saw Nessa stand and hit her head on the bubble. Good-bye to their peaceful moment. What would be coming next were not so kind words from her, so Devin pushed his hand into the tree as quickly as he could and the coldness of the tree took him.

When Devin appeared outside of Randolph Manor, he was exactly where he planned to arrive. There were very few trees he could picture on the estate, but luckily there was one that he could remember which was close to the house. He still had not a clue how the tree travel thing worked exactly, but it did, and for that he was grateful.

Quietly, Devin walked the few feet to the backdoor that used to be his home. It was the servants' quarters, but Devin had always felt more comfortable there than up above in the main part of the house with Arianna Grace, the heir to the Randolph estate. This was the normal section of the manor, and Lord Randolph—and now Arianna—lived in the extravagant part. Devin wasn't avoiding Arianna, but rather knew where he would find the man he needed to see.

Devin entered the empty hallway and made his way to his old quarters. It was strange to be back. It still seemed the same, but in reality it was different. Home, but not quite home anymore. Devin paused outside of the door to the apartment he'd shared with Arianna's protection team. They would be wherever Arianna was, so they were not home … at least not everyone. He knew Mori would be around. There was no way Mori would be anywhere but with his computer. He essentially lived in his room.

Crossing the front room, he only stopped briefly to look

around. He had spent years here, but it just didn't feel the same as it once did. Devin knocked on the closed door off the living room, but no one answered. Devin knocked again. Still there was no answer.

Devin slowly pushed open the door and let the light from the living room creep into the dark bedroom. He wasn't about to barge into the room. Mori was still a night human, after all, and not worth startling to the point that he instinctively attacked. A young Asian guy glanced up from the computer, the only source of light in the room. Startled, he pushed back his headphones and grinned.

"It's been only a few days. Missed us that much that you rushed back? It's too bad Arianna isn't here," he responded. "That didn't take long at all. Guess Nessa was right about knowing how to break a bond. Always thought she didn't have a clue, but guess not, huh?"

"Not quite," Devin replied. Confused, Mori stared at Devin.

"Not quite what?" he asked. Mori was one that liked puzzles, but he liked having direct information just as much.

"Seems like you can't break a bond that works," Devin replied with a shrug. There wasn't much more of an explanation he could give. Devin was bonded to Nessa, and the bond was for life.

"Then you're not back?" Mori asked, sounding a bit disappointed. Devin was the only one that Mori regularly spoke more than a few words to at one time.

"I don't think I'll ever really be back," Devin replied, putting the news out there as quickly as possible.

"Not coming back? Like ever?" Mori asked.

"Like short-term visits only," Devin replied. "I'm kind of stuck there now. I'm still human, yet kind of sidhe." Devin let the late kings' power flow through his veins, and the swords appeared on his back. Mori would like that one. He was a wealth of knowledge and always wanted to learn new things. Devin was a new *thing*.

Mori stood up and scurried over to Devin, inspecting the swords. When he came back to face Devin, he looked directly at where the dead king had placed the stone inside of his chest cavity, making Devin like the sidhe. Mori had already used his night human senses to analyze Devin.

"What is that?" Mori asked, pointing to the spot.

"No clue. Some sort of power transfer that lets me use all of the late king's powers. It makes me one of them; technically, I can do anything a sidhe can do. I have no clue how it works, and I doubt anyone there knows, either," Devin explained, letting the swords fade away.

"And instant blades? How cool is that?" Mori asked, watching them fade with a hint on envy in his voice. Devin was unsure if he was referring to the swords, which would be silly as Mori never left this room beyond going to the lab, or for the knowledge as to how to bundle night human abilities into one small thing and place it inside of a day human. It was probably the latter.

"I didn't come back to stay or say good-bye," Devin stated, restarting the conversation to keep on track. By now Nessa had to be fuming because Devin was taking too long. Even with hundreds of miles separating them, Devin could feel the bond. She wasn't at the point of exploding, but she was mad. "I came back to see if you can do me a favor."

"Sure, anything," Mori replied, still staring at the spot in Devin chest, as if it would give him answers.

"I need these samples analyzed." Devin held up the vials of poison he had removed from the various people in the past twenty-four hours. Mori took them and began to uncap the first one. "Be careful with those. They are a poison, a quick-acting one." Mori didn't finish uncapping the tube. Instead, he held them up to the light of his computer and stared at them some more, stopping on the last one.

"And a toe?" Mori asked.

"Couldn't get the poison out of it," Devin replied.

"So these are different poisons?" Mori asked, glancing between the vials.

"I'm not sure. I thought they were the same, but something is different with the last ones. They were harder to get out of the people, and the toe one I couldn't remove any of it. Rolf said it was a poison called clauthau, but he has no clue what it is, or where it comes from. Any information would help. I pulled the first sample from Nessa yesterday," Devin explained, which clarified why he was there now.

"I'll take it to the lab right away," Mori replied. He understood the urgency of Nessa's poisoning. Devin was bonded to her, and if she died, then Devin would die also.

"Thanks," Devin replied, turning to leave.

"It should take about two to three hours," Mori added. "You might want to call in a friend to help track it." Mori was always quick to come up with solutions.

Devin paused. "Who would you suggest?" Devin didn't know anyone else he should ask for help.

"I know of a particular hound-like person who's bored out of his mind now that he isn't needed. Andrew is more than capable of protecting Arianna on his own, and it's not like she's let out of his view ever. The rest of the guys are a bit bored." Mori followed Devin back into the living room, squinting from the bright light of the dim lamp in the room.

Devin nodded. That wasn't a bad idea. Once in the hallway, Devin moved to the door exiting the mansion, and Mori turned to walk further in. Devin felt he should say something. It wasn't like he was leaving them behind forever, but it would be different. Things were changing.

"You may be one of them now, but that doesn't mean we still aren't family. If you need anything, we're here for you," Mori called as he walked away. Mori was strange. He was as introverted as one could get, but somehow knew exactly what Devin needed to hear.

He smiled at the retreating dearg-dul. They had been his family since he was a child, but Nessa had grown on him. There was something special about her, he just couldn't pinpoint what it was that he liked about her. There wasn't one big thing, but rather a lot of little things. He couldn't leave her now—even if the bond was broken—she was his family.

Devin made it back to the tree and traveled to the parked car he'd left outside of the sidhe village days ago. His baby was sitting there, gathering dust. Being inside of the spacious dearg-dul manor had been strange, but now even his car seemed a bit out of place. He had gone days without any modern technology, and now he was back to it. He could understand Nessa's confusion and awe of the outside world. It was different, but that didn't make it wrong. It would have been a lot easier to walk into a fully functional lab in the village and have his samples analyzed rather than traveling across the country to get Mori to do it. There had to be a middle ground.

As he opened his car door, he pulled out his cell phone. It was still almost fully charged. At least that was a good thing, since it wasn't like there was electricity anywhere nearby, and he didn't want to have to sit in his car and wait to get a charge. Nessa was already nearing her breaking point waiting for him. Devin flipped open the phone and made his call. He didn't doubt Turner would come to help. He had been Devin's only friend over the years, and the best guy to call for a bit of danger. Turner loved an adventure, and the sidhe would provide exactly that.

Nessa hit the bubble once more. She didn't have time to waste sitting around in a bubble. There were still more complaints she had to hear today, and she had to deal with Fiona … or rather, Maureen. Nessa still had no clue about what to do about that. Nessa had no doubts that Fiona was carrying her dead brother's child, but she couldn't validate that without losing the throne herself. Nessa didn't want to be queen, but she really didn't want Maureen getting control of the sidhe, either. If Maureen was willing to kill Nessa for the throne, Nessa didn't want to see what she'd be willing to do to the sidhe people who didn't follow her orders, or to her unborn nephew. Nessa was caught in a hard situation. Either way, she couldn't win. Deny the child, and never know her nephew; acknowledge the child, and lose the throne to Maureen and her evils.

'Where are you?' Nessa finally complained. It had been over fifteen minutes already.

'Coming back now,' Devin replied, not answering the question.

Devin walked out of the same tree he had left from. Nessa was shocked, but covered it with her anger. Every tree on the palace grounds had been stunted to not allow travel, since they couldn't have people able to travel by the trees into the palace; it would make the palace unsafe. How could Devin travel without using a tree? Nessa was sure none of the trees worked for leaving or coming, as she had tried all of them herself over time when she wanted to get away. It wasn't until she followed Rhys once that she learned she could leave by one gate entrance in particular; never had she seen him use the trees. She had no clue how Devin could.

"Your grandfather planted this tree," Devin told her, answering her thoughts. Nessa pouted. She didn't want answers. Well, she did, but she was still mad, and still sitting in a bubble. "He made it so that only he could come and go through it. Since I have his powers and your blood, I figured it would work for me as well. Guess it does."

Devin reached forward and broke the bubble. Nessa immediately stood and slapped him.

"Stop doing that to me. Have you ever thought maybe I'd need to go pee or something?" she scolded him.

"You could have told me. I said I could come back at any moment," Devin replied with a smile. That wasn't the true reason she was mad, but the thought had crossed his mind. If she did really need to go, she would have been even madder once he arrived.

Nessa hated that smile. It made her forgive him, and she didn't want to.

"So did you figure out what you needed to do?" she asked, curious to where he went, but not about to ask. She didn't want to be feeling all of the conflicted feelings she felt.

"Yes," Devin replied, not giving any more information. She hated that about him. He could be tight-lipped if he wanted.

Nessa stormed ahead and shoved open the door to her room. Catching a glimpse into the side room where Gemma and Ronan still slept, she paused, seeing her uncle was still sitting with them. He stood as they entered and nodded to both Nessa and Devin. His fear of Devin seemed to have faded away somewhat since Devin had saved his children.

"What are we supposed to do now?" Nessa asked as Rolf joined them. "We can't have the other sidhe come here for the coronation if there's someone shooting darts that kill in minutes."

Rolf nodded. "If we lose any of them in our village, there will be war between the clans."

"You war amongst yourselves even?" Devin asked.

The dearg-dul clan Devin had come from was a more of a standard monarchy where Lord Randolph ruled over them all. No one would go against his will, and his say was final. There were never wars between the dearg-dul clans. Even though Nessa would soon be queen, Devin wasn't sure how much power she actually had.

"While our family might be the rulers, each village is governed by one of the head families," Rolf replied. "Fighting between villages is as common as fights here in the palace. The families have never gotten along. Any excuse to battle is one that everyone agrees to play."

The situation was bad, but her uncle's description was making it worse. Not everyone got along, but every visit she'd ever had to the other villages was never one of danger. She enjoyed seeing all of the other towns. Nessa was beginning to see just how sheltered she was. She was stuck, and not prepared to handle it all. Nessa again realized how strongly she didn't want to be queen, but what options were left?

Devin reached over and took her hand. Her emotions leaked through the bond because she didn't bother to try to hide them from him. What was the point? They were in the center of it, and she was sure this was just the beginning. They were never going to have a quiet, peaceful life, but that didn't matter to him. She was strong enough, and they would make it through it all together.

"We take this one problem at a time. I have someone helping on the poisons and tracking down the person making it. If we stop it being made, we stop people dying. If we are lucky, we can even find the person using it. Right now I think we need to change and get ready for the day. You still have more on your list to listen to, right?" Devin asked.

Devin was calm and confident, which was exactly what Nessa needed. It didn't seem to rattle him at all that their lives were in constant danger. Nessa had no clue how he could be peaceful in this situation; it was beginning to wear on her. What sort of life had he lived before she met him? Had his life always been like this?

Rolf nodded at Devin's words. He was ready to let Devin take charge, and knew that Devin was who they needed. He was strong and wouldn't waver. Nessa could see it, too. Devin seemed to thrive under pressure.

"You stay here in case either of them wake," Devin told Rolf. "I'll be with Nessa."

"But what if we need help?" Nessa asked. "It's not like I know the laws too well, and I doubt you've had time to study all of them all."

Grinning, Devin pulled her back to the bedroom, away from her uncle. Nessa didn't understand why, but she went along with him.

"Why would I need to know the laws when I can tell if someone is lying?" Nessa's mouth hung open. She was unsure if he was kidding or not, but that wasn't something she wanted him to be able to do. "And if I need any law advice, I'll just ask your uncle. I can talk to any sidhe mentally, just like I talk with you."

"How?" she asked, suspicious of the lying bit. She already knew he was connected to the sidhe like she was, and that she didn't need to have her uncle present to ask him questions, but his physical being was nice to have around to draw on, as he was almost as confident as Devin was in public.

Devin shrugged and shut the bedroom door. "It was one of those powers of your grandfather's. Not quite sure how it works, but I do know. When people lie, I can just tell that it's not true."

"Not possible," she whispered. She hoped he was kidding, because she didn't want him being able to tell when she was lying. That would make life much more complicated.

"I can prove it," Devin replied with a grin. He took a step back and Nessa finally noticed he had her trapped with the closed door behind her.

"How?" she squeaked. He was making it impossible to be mad at him when he gave her the sultry look he was giving now.

"Do you want me to kiss you?" he asked.

Nessa wasn't prepared for that question. Did she? Yes, of course. Would she admit that? Not a chance. She was supposed to still be mad at him. "No," she answered, keeping her features calm and straight-faced as she had been taught.

"You're lying," Devin replied, stepping closer. One arm looped around her waist and pulled her to him, positioning his face beside hers. "Do you want me to ask another question? Was that one not fair?"

"No," she quickly replied. If he could really tell when she was lying, then she wasn't sure she wanted to answer anything he asked.

"See? It's not that hard to tell the truth," he whispered in her ear, sending tingles down her legs.

Devin slowly pulled back slowly. When he gazed into her eyes, Nessa held her breath. She wanted him to kiss her, and it took all of her restraint to keep from throwing herself at him. It wasn't fair. Devin could read her emotions and her thoughts, and if she tried to lie he would know that, too. She was completely on the unfair side of the equation.

"You better get dressed. They should be expecting us," Devin said as he walked away.

Nessa stood in shock for a second. She was sure he was going to kiss her, but he hadn't. Guys were too confusing. Why did they have to be that way?

Turning around, Devin grinned at her. "If you want me to

kiss you, then don't lie about it," he added before walking over to his bag of clothes to get ready to meet with the elite sidhe.

Heading over to her own clothes, Nessa picked up one of his shirts that was lying over the chair next to her. She threw it at him and huffed as she walked into the bathroom.

"Thanks," he called after her. "That was just the one I was looking for."

CHAPTER 7

After another five "fun-filled" hours, Nessa sat and stared at the audience that was still waiting in the amphitheater. All of her cases, beyond Fiona's second chance to speak, were done. There was no need for everyone to stick around, but the drama of Fiona's case would keep them all glued to their seats like day humans when they watched reality television. Unless there was more that Maureen had found overnight, there was nothing that would change with what Rolf had already said. Maureen needed a miracle at this point. Even without new details, Maureen was going to show up. She never backed down from a challenge. Just spreading the rumor alone, that the late king had an heir, would damage Nessa's claim to the throne. Nessa didn't want to deal with the headache the Ferguson family brought, but it was her last case. She needed to be done with it in order to move on with preparations for the coronation. She didn't want to sit in the room listening to complaints any longer.

Maureen stood and approached the stage. She moved slowly, and allowed everyone to take in her ornate dress. Her head was held tall, and she didn't look at anyone but Nessa as she walked gracefully past the rest of the sidhe. Everything about her said she was playing the part of future grandmother to the queen. She was in theatrical production mode, and planning to make a grand plea of her case.

Nessa rolled her eyes, and Devin coughed to cover a laugh. They might not get along all the time, but they were in agreement when it came to Maureen.

"Next up, Maureen Ferguson," Devin announced, still coughing a little. "Anything new you'd like to add today? I'm pretty sure your case was decided yesterday."

"I brought the two witnesses to the wedding," Maureen explained, motioning for two people to join her.

'They are elders in the Ferguson family. They are witnesses for the clan, and cannot tell a lie,' Nessa told him. It wasn't good to see that Maureen had brought elders. By law, they could not lie to the courts, and were to oversee all arrangements of the family. Either they were really married, or the elders were going to commit a crime against their position. Nessa didn't know which, but both were not good.

Devin nodded to Nessa as he looked at each man. He was already prepared for the liars.

"Before I ask them to tell me what they came here to say, I'd first like to reiterate to everyone sitting here that I have been given *all* of the powers of the former king," Devin said loudly enough for the room to hear him. Most of the people stared back blankly at Devin, but the two elders flinched as the crossed swords appeared on Devin's back. "I don't know how the man did it, but he did. Those powers are inside of me now, and will be for the rest of my life. Included in those powers is the ability to tell when one lies to me. So please step forward to tell the truth."

The room erupted into chaos. Obviously only the older people in the room knew of that power. The younger were all as shocked and dismayed as Nessa was. She didn't doubt him now, not because of his display before they arrived, but because he would openly admit it to the room. If he had any doubts on that power, he wouldn't have said anything. Devin was always calculated in every risk he took. If he admitted to a room that he could do something, he would be able to do it perfectly. Nessa never once saw him claim to do something without being able to do it better than anyone expected. That was Devin's style.

Devin smiled as the two men with Maureen pulled her back to talk to her. His statement would cause a stir. It might have been better to not let people know—then he could have used it in secret—but he needed them to understand when he told them the truth about the supposed wedding of Fiona and Rhys. Either way, Devin needed the elite sidhe there to believe him. Nessa completely understood and was proud of him. Devin was meant to be a leader.

'What is the punishment if they are caught lying in public events?' Devin questioned her.

'Exiled to the castoffs camp for them and their entire immediate family,' Nessa replied. The elders were exalted members of their family, and took an oath to not lie. Nessa had never heard of one lying before, but then again, this would be just their word against Devin's. Nessa knew that is why Maureen was using them. An elder's word against a day human. She was sure who everyone would believe, but not sure that they would support the elders now if Devin said they were lying.

Maureen seemed to be upset by what the men were telling her. They were quietly arguing when Devin stopped them.

"Now, what would you two gentlemen like to add to the debate? We decided yesterday that there's no contest to the throne at this time, even if this is the former king's child. The child will be a bastard and has no claim to the throne," Devin reiterated to the gathered crowd that was finally quieting. Devin seemed to know exactly how to play the game; he was challenging the two men to lie to him.

"They would both like to confirm that Fiona and King Rhys were married," Maureen spoke for the two men, who seemed to have lost their nerve. She was still willing to take her chance.

"That's nice, but they need to be the ones to say that to be entered into the court documents." Devin motioned to the young sidhe that was transcribing the events. They needed to speak for Devin to tell if they were telling the truth or not.

Nessa gave Devin a questioning look. How did he know how to play the game of sidhe politics so well? In answer to her question, Devin tilted his head toward the back of the room. Uncle Rolf was by the doorway. Nessa nodded in understanding. While she had not seen him enter, she was grateful for her uncle and his knowledge. Nessa needed him now more than ever. Never once, when skipping lessons on sidhe law for combat lessons, had she thought that maybe her fate depended on knowing those laws.

'Gemma is awake and fine. She is sitting with Ronan right now,' Devin explained.

Nessa smiled and felt as though a weight lifted off her chest. However, she was still very worried about her cousins. She didn't want to lose the last family she had. Maureen saw Nessa's smile and scowled, thinking it was because the older lady was caught. Her two witnesses didn't seem to want to speak. Devin coughed over a chuckle again.

'Why is she mad at me? What did I do now?' Nessa asked, truly confused.

'Timing, love, timing,' Devin replied, while keeping his face serious. She could feel the humor in his voice, but externally he was completely composed. Devin was definitely well-trained in the art of night human politics.

"Well, we can't wait around all day. We have a coronation

to get ready for, and I have a few leads on the assassin to take care of in the meantime." Devin looked straight at Maureen. Nessa got the hint behind his words and look. Maureen didn't flinch, but stared back defiantly. She had been playing the game longer than Devin, and was equally prepared.

'Is she part of the assassination attempt?' Nessa asked. That had not crossed her mind. Yes, Maureen tried once before to kill Nessa, but with Devin's threat of disbanding the entire family of the one at fault, Nessa thought there was no way possible Maureen would chance it. Her family, and the power of her family, was everything for her.

'I'm not sure, but hers is the only family that has not been attacked. I'd say she's most likely involved,' Devin replied while continuing his stare down with Maureen. The odds were against her, after all. Nessa had not been keeping track, but Devin was right. Maureen's family was the only one without an attack.

Devin looked to each Ferguson elder, and both stared helplessly at him. "Do either of you have anything to say?"

Both men vehemently shook their heads. Smiling, Devin nodded. His threat was enough to keep them to their job. Nessa had a feeling Devin might have actually just made things a bit easier for himself. The sidhe may fear him, and now have more fear, but he'd pretty much guaranteed they weren't going to lie to him. He hated the deception and games, and that would have to be a relief for him.

"Then the case is closed. Without a marriage, whether or not Rhys was the father of Fiona's child doesn't matter. The child will be a Ferguson, and thus not in line for the throne. It remains that Vanessa will be made queen with Ronan McKinny second in line until she produces an heir of her own." Devin stood and offered his hand to Nessa. He was happy to be finished with the elite. Nessa could feel the happiness roll off of him.

'And just like that, we are done,' Devin told Nessa.

Devin winked at her as they walked past the fuming Maureen. Nessa could almost see the relief in Fiona's eyes. As conniving as Fiona could be, she might not have been following her mother by choice. Nessa couldn't help but feel sorry for her. It seemed that for once she might have been caught in the web of her mother's games.

Devin paused at the doorway to their apartment. Nessa walked inside, but immediately turned and crossed her arms with a pout. She'd gotten the hint and knew that he was going to lock her inside again. She wasn't happy about it.

"You're not coming in?" she asked accusingly.

"I need to go pick someone up outside the village," Devin replied. Hating his vague answer, Nessa glared at him.

"And I suppose I'm to stay here like a good girl." She was back to showing her harshness only minutes after her lightheartedness in dealing with Maureen. Devin was beginning to see a trend, and it might have been partially his fault that Nessa was an emotional rollercoaster.

"That would be the plan," Devin stated, already encasing the room in his protective bubble.

"Do you think I can't help?" Nessa murmured. Now hurt was the emotion she was emitting. Devin was having a hard time keeping up with her. The bond alone was jumping with emotions, and her voice echoed it. She was too confusing sometimes.

"That isn't it at all," Devin replied, grabbing her hands before she could pull further away from him. "I know you could help me. It would probably even go faster if I had your help, but I can't risk it. I can't have you out there exposed and risk you getting hurt. Someone still wants to kill you. I am not a sidhe. I'm not a target, but you are. If I have to sit and worry about you, then I won't be able to get done what needs to be done. I love you, Nessa."

"Are you calling me a distraction?" Nessa asked. Devin couldn't tell if that offended her, or made her happy.

"Gods, yes, you are a distraction," Devin replied. *Wasn't that obvious by now?* "Have you not figured that out yet? When you're around, I can't focus on anything else."

Nessa leaned forward and kissed him. Wrapping her arms around him, she held on tight as he responded. His hands moved to her hips and held her as close as he could get her against him. It wasn't the response he expected, as the last few times he'd tried to protect her had made her mad, but he wasn't about to complain. When she pulled back far too early, he gazed into her eyes. She truly wasn't mad this time. It was there on the tip of his tongue, what he needed to ask her, but the moment was lost as she stepped back.

"Then stay safe, and I'll wait," Nessa told him, gently pushing him out of the protective spell around her room.

Devin stood in the doorway and watched as she walked away. She was going to check on her cousin. He could feel the heartbeat of the sidhe in the room, and knew Ronan was alive but still not awake. Devin was sorry he had to cut off his two toes, but Ronan would be thankful to not be dead once he woke, and hopefully would not care too much.

With Nessa in a good mood for a change, Devin relaxed slightly as he made his way out of the palace and into the village. He planned to go by foot instead of the trees to meet Turner because he wasn't sure where he would find him. He had told Turner where his car was parked. It would have been nice if Turner would wait there, but Devin knew his friend all too well. Turner wouldn't just sit and wait. He wasn't a patient guy. With his great lycan sense of smell, Turner was sure to come wandering into the village, if he could get that far.

Devin paused at the edge of the town. It was still magical how everything fit with nature, but something had changed now that he knew they hid people off in the shadows because they didn't fit perfectly into their sidhe world. All of the castoff families he had stopped by at the start of the day were just that: families. He had expected castoffs to be more like prisoners and bad people. A typical castoff committed a crime, and therefore couldn't be a part of regular society. Yet, there wasn't a single bad person there. They deserved more, and Devin couldn't wait to help them after he settled everything with the assassin and Nessa's coronation.

As Devin crossed the bridge into the village, he found Lindsey standing in the clearing. Lindsey was the keeper of the sidhe; he guarded the one road into the village and was always on alert. As Devin approached, the hulking, green, moss-covered giant turned slightly to him.

"Hello, Day Human Prince," Lindsey called in his booming voice. The man was twice the size of the largest man Devin had ever seen. Days ago, when he'd first met him, Devin had been shocked. Even now, having seen him before, he was still stunned to be standing in his presence.

"I didn't figure I'd catch you up and about," Devin replied, thinking how he never even saw the old sidhe when he first walked into that same clearing with Nessa days ago. He was first deceived as the giant sat in disguise, and secondly because Devin couldn't track the man because he moved quicker than the wind.

"We have a visitor coming, and he's coming quickly. I figured best to be prepared," Lindsey explained. He was doing his job.

Devin smiled. "Is it in the form of a night human?" Devin asked, guessing Turner was on his way.

"A hairy night human," Lindsey replied with some disgust. "I'm not fond of dogs."

Devin laughed. Turner's lycan form was hairy, whether he was partially or fully transformed. He didn't recall the phase of the moon, but either way, Lindsey's description would be correct. "I'll greet this one." Lindsey looked back at Devin and nodded.

"As you wish, Prince." Lindsey bowed and moved to the side of the clearing. The old giant sat down and blended right in with the scenery as if that was where he always sat. The moss on him matched the moss on the neighboring trees.

Devin moved back to the bridge and waited as Turner approached. Half human, half wolf, Turner ran into the clearing. It must have been between moons after all. Turner paused, surrounded by the grass. He turned first to where Lindsey was sitting blended into the nature around him. Then Turner turned to Devin, letting his night human side go. He shook from head to toe as the hair faded, and he became a man. Turner flashed his brilliantly white smile while shaking his reddish-brown locks when he laughed. Devin hopped down and met Turner in the middle of the glade. It had been only a few days, but since they had spent more than the last year together—almost constantly—protecting Arianna, it was a long time apart. Especially when you were used to seeing and arguing with someone all day, every day.

"I was almost thinking you just set this up as an elaborate game, and wouldn't be here when I arrived," Turner said as he grasped Devin's arm to shake it.

"You really think I'd do this to entertain you?" Devin asked. Driving to the middle of nowhere, hiking to the middle of nowhere, and then leaving sounded like a time-consuming hoax. It was definitely something Turner would have done—but that was more his style—not Devin. Smiling, Turner shrugged; he was probably storing it in his book of pranks for the future.

"It has gotten quite boring at the Randolph estate," Turner replied. "I know you were busy when you were with us days ago, but I'm going crazy. Figured you had to have noticed that much, and were offering to entertain me."

Devin hadn't realized that before he left. He had been a little busy noticing Nessa, or trying to not notice Nessa, to pay attention to the lack of work. Devin was sure that Turner was right. Arianna's bonded night human was one of the strongest Devin had encountered in a long time. She was perfectly safe and didn't need her keepers now.

"I talked to Mori on the way. He said he needs another couple of hours for whatever you have him doing," Turner continued, oblivious to Devin not replying the first time. This time Turner paused for Devin to speak.

"Glad you could make it so fast," Devin answered. "Sorry, this isn't a hoax. I really need some help."

"Of course! What do you need me for?" Turner asked. "The sooner I get this done, the sooner we can return and find something else to do because it is so boring there now." Turner looked around the glen. "And where would your little night human be now? I figured she'd not let you out of her sight since you said the bond wasn't broken yet."

"Yeah, 'bout that ..." Devin tried to figure out the best way to tell Turner. It had been easy to tell Mori he wasn't coming back because he understood what the bond meant. Unfortunately, Turner had no clue about the bond.

"What?" Turner asked, looking into the forest for Nessa. "Is she hiding somewhere, and I have offended her?"

Laughing, Devin shook his head. It was a perfectly fine assessment of her, and she wouldn't be offended in the least.

"About the coming home part," Devin began again. He

wasn't used to the energy that Turner emitted. It was strange to now be able to see him in the light that the sidhe would. He was as close to nature as they were, possibly even more so since he turned into a wolf during a full moon. He fit in with the sidhe world, yet was as different and foreign as Devin was. "I'm not going back to Arianna."

Turner stared at Devin, obviously trying to make sense of his words. Everyone still expected Devin to return because he hadn't had time to tell most of his family and friends. Arianna obviously hadn't shared it with the team. Turner shook his head and opened his mouth to speak.

"You heard correct," Devin replied before Turner could get a word out. "I'm not going back. I have to stay here. I'm kind of one of them now."

"She turned you?" Turner's eyes bugged out of his head as his form flickered between his normal human form and his night human form. Anger was rising in the lycan.

"No, no," Devin quickly replied, holding his hands up in surrender and trying to calm his friend. "No one turned me. I'm still a day human."

"They why can't you leave?" Turner asked. He needed more information, and Devin was not doing the best to calm him down. His night human form flickered a second time.

"First off, because I'm still bonded to her," Devin replied. Turner once again moved to speak, and Devin held up his hand. "It can't be broken. If the bond really forms, you can't break it, ever. I'm connected to Nessa for life. My life and hers will be forever intertwined, and she belongs here. I can't leave."

"But she said—" Turner got in before he continued.

Devin shook his head. "She thought she could, but it's not possible. I'm bonded to her. Second is, while I am still a day human, I'm part of the sidhe now," Devin replied. He didn't know how to explain it without a play-by-play account of his time since he'd gotten there. Turner would eventually get it out of Devin, but there were more pressing matters. "I can't just leave them. Being bonded to Nessa kind of made me a sidhe prince."

Turner stared at Devin, taking in his serious face, and broke out in laughter. Devin allowed him to get it out of his system. However, when Turner realized Devin wasn't laughing, his merriment stopped and he looked up at Devin.

"You're serious?" Turner asked in shock, not knowing what else to say. The best friend that had left Turner only days ago, talked about coming back in less than a week. This Devin talked about never coming back.

"Dead serious," Devin replied. He didn't want to leave his friends and family. However, since he was not needed around Arianna anymore, he had already been planning on leaving for a while. Initially, Nessa had been a good excuse to leave, and now she was a great one to stay away.

Turner's face fell. That was not what he was expecting to hear. The lycan was shocked into silence. As soft as the wind through the trees, Devin could hear Lindsey laughing. It wasn't funny either way. It was just the truth, and he couldn't expect Turner to understand completely ... he had never been bonded to someone before.

"You're never coming back?" Turner asked, hurt lacing his voice. "You're just giving Arianna up?"

"I can come and visit, but I must live here now," Devin replied. He'd never let his intentions of leaving be known to everyone before. "And Arianna made her choice. She has Andrew now. She doesn't need me."

"You're really going to do this? You want to stay here?" Turner asked, looking around the empty glen.

Devin shrugged. "It isn't really a choice now. I love Nessa." Devin was shocked that he'd actually admitted that much. He hated how Turner could get things like that out of him.

Shaking his head, Turner smiled at him. That statement was enough to convince him that Devin needed to stay. Turner understood love. "Then I guess you stay. Why'd you call me here? It isn't like you need my approval."

"No. I need the bloodhound in you, actually," Devin replied with a shrug.

Turner shook his head; he hated being called a dog. "I'm not a bloodhound, or a pet for hire." Turner walked a few steps away from Devin and quickly turned to attack. However, a large, green-tinged hand was in Devin's place and held tight to Turner's much smaller hand. "What the …"

"Oh, I forgot to mention. This here is Lindsey. He's a bit protective over the sidhe, and since I am one now, I guess he's protective of me as well," Devin explained. He didn't actually expect Lindsey to defend him, but it was nice to know that the giant considered Devin part of the village, even if he was still a day human. "I suppose you should let him go. He always tries to get the best of me. He hasn't won yet, and we kind of need his help."

Lindsey let go, but did not move. He stood defensively between Devin and Turner. The sidhe wasn't going to take any chances. The large, green giant sized up the smaller lycan. It would be a great fight to watch. He almost didn't want to interrupt.

"Must I test him to see if he's worthy to enter?" Lindsey asked Devin.

"Can I test him?" Devin suggested. It would be fun to watch, but just as much fun to test all of his new sidhe skills. There was no one in the village or palace that would even think of sparing with Devin. This was too good of a chance to pass up.

Lindsey bowed his head. "As you wish, Day Human

Prince."

"Prince? Really?" Turner replied, mocking Devin.

Devin shrugged. He was getting used to the title and the way everyone treated him. He'd prefer to be a regular person, but it was nothing he could change. Nessa was the princess, and she was his.

"So what is this test?" Turner asked. "I didn't have time to study."

"You never study," Devin replied. Turner was one of the biggest slackers when it came to school that Devin had ever met. In fact, Devin was surprised he had graduated from high school. Turner grinned and didn't deny the assessment. "Besides, this is more of a physical test."

"You mean we get to spar?" Turner asked, his eyes lighting up with surprise, happy for the chance.

"Oh yes, spar. But let me tell you—" Devin began, but was interrupted as Turner moved to strike him. Devin blocked the blow easily and moved back to continue talking. "Things aren't the same now. I've had a bit of a change in my life. I'm way too far out of your league."

"We'll see about that," Turner replied. "You're not the only one who has been practicing."

"Yeah. Practicing isn't exactly what I've been doing," Devin replied, letting the sidhe magic flow in his veins. The double swords appeared on his back. "More like getting an upgrade."

Turner's eyes popped open at the sight of the swords. Sidhe magic filled the glen. Devin was ready to test out his new powers. Turner didn't have a quick comeback this time; it was obvious that Devin was now out of his league. Devin grinned at his oldest friend. He'd play nice, but that didn't mean he wasn't going to have some fun beating on Turner.

CHAPTER 8

Turner rubbed his jaw as they walked over the bridge into the sidhe village. Devin had been nice and only hurt him as much as he could instantly heal. Night humans were always fun to spar against for that reason alone. Turner hadn't even seen most of the moves as they came. The power between the two friends was once almost equal, but now they were too far apart; Devin was in a class of his own. Turner rubbed his face again. The jaw would feel fine in a few minutes.

"You really meant that stuff about being a sidhe now," Turner said as they entered the first street. He was coming to terms with what Devin had told him.

"Oh, yes. The old king put all of his powers in me without actually changing me into a sidhe. I get all of the powers, but don't have to drink blood to support them," Devin replied, nodding to Old Man Winters as they passed. The old man nodded back as he walked beside his horse, which was pulling the cart. "Night human abilities with a day human life… guess it's the best of both worlds." Devin hadn't thought hard about it, but that was the best description.

All around them sidhe were busy with their day ending, and Devin was walking a new night human through the reclusive town. Faces turned to them as they passed, and many stopped what they were doing to study them. No one said anything, but they did watch. The sidhe didn't have many visitors, and probably none that were walking together. A day human and a lycan walking together through the sidhe village was probably a first for these people.

"Why do I feel like I'm on display?" Turner whispered. He had noticed the visible attention.

"Because we are," Devin replied. "They don't get out much around here. Can't you tell? You instantly became the most interesting man in the village. Too bad they don't marry outside of the sidhe. You'd be the most eligible bachelor, with hundreds of options."

Turner puffed out his chest a bit more as they walked. He might have said he didn't like to be on display, but Devin knew otherwise. Turner liked any sort of attention—good or bad. Devin was just boosting his ego when he explained it to him, and he knew the affect it would have. He preferred his friend to have confidence in this situation, and it would make his life easier back at the palace if Turner was confident.

Devin made his way through town, and it was an easy, direct walk to the palace. Everyone moved out of their way as they encountered the sidhe. The female sidhe seemed especially interested in the strange night human. It wasn't like they had much of a selection in the city when they were forced to stay within their families. Devin made it to the palace garden walls and began to lead the way around to the one entrance he could go in undetected. Finally, at the right one, they entered.

"What? You're too good to use the other entrances? Is this the life of a prince? You get your own doorway?" Turner asked, noticing their walk past the others.

"You should know," Devin replied. Turner's father was a ruler of another night human town. While Turner was second in line to his father, behind his older brother, he did live a life of privilege way beyond what Devin ever had.

Devin led the way into the palace, to where he was sure Nessa would be anxiously waiting. She had to have known by now who Devin invited, but she was silent across the bond.

"Is everything like this?" Turner asked as he stopped. Devin turned back around.

"Like what?" Devin asked in return. He didn't know what Turner was talking about.

"This," Turner said as he kicked the dirt ground. It was well-tread and patted down solidly, but it was still a dirt path inside of the palace.

Devin smiled and nodded. It had seemed strange to him also when he'd first arrived, but now he didn't even notice. The natural world around him was just that now: the world around him.

"Yes, hence the reason I needed Mori's help. Do you think they have any real scientific equipment around here?" Devin replied, and Turner nodded in agreement. Devin opened the door to Nessa's room.

Devin walked in, surprised to find Nessa not in the main room. He looked to the side and the open doorway to discover the cause: Ronan was finally awake. Devin went straight to where Nessa was sitting on one side of Ronan, and Gemma on the other side of her brother. Turner stayed in the doorway.

"Hey, Devin," Ronan called to him as Devin entered. "Thanks for the save."

Devin shook his head. Ronan seemed completely healed from the poison and back to good spirits. He was talking like Devin just made a play in a game, not that his life was in the balance or anything.

"Sorry about the toes," Devin replied. He was truly sorry he couldn't get the poison completely out of him. Ronan was a good guy, and Devin felt like he had maimed the young man, even if it was just a few toes to save his life. "It was take the toes, or let the poison take you. I really didn't want to have to do that, but your father assured me that the poison wouldn't come out no matter what I tried."

"Ahh, I was thinking just the other day that I could do without a few toes. I don't need to count to twenty, anyway. Besides, it makes me more mysterious," Ronan joked. Nessa hit his shoulder as he laughed.

"You are supposed to be resting," she complained. Gemma nodded, her face laced with concern.

"I have been resting. What do you call sleeping all day?" Ronan replied, nudging Nessa to make her fall off the bed.

Nessa stood up and dusted herself off, finally looking at Devin in the process. Her stare quickly turned to Turner in the doorway. She hadn't noticed who Devin had brought into the village after all. Devin was thankful that Ronan recovered and could be such a good distraction.

"I take it this is the help you called in?" Nessa asked.

Gemma and Ronan also looked past Devin now. Gemma blushed and glanced back at her brother. Devin was sure he was the first non-sidhe she had met, and now Turner was the second.

"Brought friends to play? I'm passed out for just a day and you have to replace me," Ronan said, pretending to be hurt.

Devin shook his head, glad that Ronan was obviously going to be completely fine.

"This is Turner," Devin introduced him for Gemma and Ronan. "He's a lycan, and I figured would be my best help in finding the assassins."

"Any help is appreciated," Ronan replied, still in good spirits. "I only have eight toes left, so I can't get hit too many more times. It probably would be better to get someone with more toes." This time Gemma hit her brother. Ronan only laughed.

"Glad to see you're fine," Devin told Ronan before turning to leave with Turner.

Nessa follow Devin into the living room.

"Are you leaving again?" she asked.

Devin hated to worry her, but he needed to find out who the assassins were. He was sure they weren't done, and when they came back, Nessa would probably be at the top of the hit list. He turned to her and took her hands in his own.

"I promise to be safe," Devin replied. "And I'm sorry to say it again, but I just need you to stay here safe as well. No matter what Ronan says, keep him here, too. You three are the last left in your family. You could all be targets."

Nessa nodded. She could tell, even without the bond, that he was filled with concern to the point that she couldn't argue.

When Devin opened the door to the apartment, Turner stepped outside. However, Nessa didn't let go of Devin's other hand; she dragged him back to her.

"You stay safe, also," she replied, pulling him down for a brief kiss.

As he moved back, Devin smiled, and thought that he could get used to the worried Nessa. Worried Nessa was actually a bit easier to deal with. She smiled as his thought crossed the bond even though he hadn't meant for it to.

"Both of you be safe," Nessa said, looking to Turner. "Welcome to my messed up home, by the way."

"Messed up?" Turner asked. "They seem like a loving bunch, all willing to kill each other off. What's family if there isn't any drama?" Turner winked at Nessa, and she nodded in reply. Drama was what the sidhe were all about. "Don't worry about your lover here." Devin smacked Turner on the back as he talked to Nessa because things weren't like that yet. "I'll keep him safe."

Nessa shut the door behind them, and Devin didn't look

back. He didn't need to since he could feel everything that Nessa was feeling. She really was worried. He thought it was silly, and if she saw how the sidhe completely ignored him she would stop. No one cared what, or where, the day human went. It gave him a sense of incognito at times, especially within the palace walls. The elite were particularly good at ignoring him, or even, for that matter, avoiding him. He wasn't worried about the assassin attacking him; he was petrified because the attack had been made on the last of the McKinny ruling family. Nessa was going to be queen soon, but Ronan was second to her, and Gemma was probably third. Someone was trying their best to change the ruling structure of the sidhe, and Devin only knew one person that desperate. Nessa, Ronan, and Gemma would be fine if they stayed in Nessa's room, and Devin sure hoped they would. His barrier would keep Nessa in because they were connected, but he was unsure if it would keep the others in.

"How long have the assassinations being going on?" Turner asked, following Devin through the hallways.

"Before we arrived, but I took care of the first ones," Devin replied.

"First ones?"

"Yeah. It started out with just attempts on Nessa. It seems not everyone wants her to be queen. Yesterday it moved on to attempts on everyone," Devin added. "What better way to stop a coronation than to make everyone afraid to come?"

"Guests are backing out?" Turner asked.

"No, not yet. We haven't told anyone outside of the palace." Devin turned again, taking them further away from Nessa, and back out the way they came.

"You're hoping you can catch this one before people arrive?" Turner asked, and Devin nodded. "When do people arrive?"

"Tomorrow, mid-day," Devin answered. He knew that it didn't give him much time, but he couldn't help it. They needed to find the assassin, and there was nothing he could do about the time table.

Turner stopped in his tracks. "We have less than twenty-four hours to find one or more assassins with a deadly poison that requires you to chop off toes to save a person?"

"Just about, but I'd like it to be faster than twenty-four hours. You know, quick enough that the person doesn't kill anyone else."

"There are already some dead?" Turner asked as they stepped out into the courtyard and exited the palace through the same door they'd entered.

Devin began to lead Turner around the palace walls again. Soon they passed by the village and were on the complete opposite side of the palace. Turner's line of thought was now fully on the mission.

"Yes," Devin finally answered. "The sidhe don't think too much of me, and a few are too proud to ask me to save their people when they are poisoned. At first it was easy to save them, but it's been getting harder. Hence the removal of toes. But it worked, so I know I can if needed."

"You can take poison out of people now? Cool new super power?" Turner deduced.

"Yes, cool new super power," Devin replied. The pathway they turned on was lit by iridescent plants that glowed in the dark night, lighting the way into the trees.

Turner walked behind Devin as he led them both further down the trail. It ended at a large, open cave. Devin hadn't been into the upper caves. His only foray into the sidhe crypt was down below only days ago, where he woke and met the former sidhe king. However, he had heard Nessa and Finn talking about the upper caves. He had traces of memories that went along with his new powers as well. Somehow, he knew exactly where to go. They walked further into the strangely lit cave, and Devin chose each turn. When they finally entered the last cavern, Devin saw the bodies of the recently dead sidhe laid out for everyone to view, and the most recent was closest to the entrance.

"This was the first one we lost," Devin explained, passing the younger bodies and stopping at the old man he'd never really met. "He was poisoned the same time as Nessa, along with these two."

Turner came closer. He bent down by the older man, but quickly backed up to sneeze. He tried again with the younger men and did the same. He looked closer at them without getting too close the third time and shook his head.

"Too much magic. It covers the scent. I can't pick up anything from them," Turner explained.

Devin nodded, as he had been afraid that would be the case. Sidhe magic covered up most everything, and therefore Devin didn't doubt that it covered scent, too. It might be nice for the sidhe to have their dead to visit for a year after their initial entombment, but it wasn't good for an investigation. No wonder the sidhe fought amongst themselves, and they continued to kill at the drop of a hat. They never knew the truth, and there was no way to find out. Another thing to change.

Nessa paced around the room as she waited. It was great that Ronan woke and was actually in good spirits after losing his toes, but she wanted to know more of what was going on, and what Devin was finding as he investigated. The bond between Nessa and Devin was as strong as ever, but she still didn't like to use it; Devin was the type of person that would share with her when he was ready. She trusted that if he found out more he would tell her, but she still worried. She had been poisoned, her cousins poisoned, and many more. Why wouldn't the person target Devin, too? Why did Devin feel confident that he was fine?

They had the new assassinations to deal with, and more would die unless they found out who it was … and soon. Because of this, it was beginning to seem like delaying the coronation would be the best route. However, that would give Maureen exactly what she wanted: more time to convince everyone to give the crown to Fiona's unborn child. The coronation had to go as planned, or else the sidhe would turn to fighting to decide what to do with Fiona and her child. Devin thought it was easily over, but it wasn't. Maureen was never going to give up. Therefore, they needed to deal with the assassins and have the coronation immediately.

Nessa walked over to the only window in the room and gazed out. People went about their daily business, none of them afraid of the new assassins, but they should have been. Nessa continued to watch, and found that she didn't recognize a single face of the people passing in the courtyard; they were all servants and commoners. Maybe that was why they weren't afraid … not a single one was elite. She was sure all of the targets were elite for a reason. Nessa envied their freedom just a bit. They were allowed to marry for love, able to choose their life and jobs. They had all of the choices Nessa never given.

What Nessa needed was a plan in order to save the remaining elite and allow the coronation to go forward. She had survived the poison once already, and with Devin around, she didn't fear it as much as he did. Yes, the poison had changed, and yes it hurt to be poisoned, but he had still saved Gemma and Ronan. She needed to do something, and if she was really the target, wouldn't it be easy to set a trap? Nessa began to picture it in her mind. If Devin would just let his guard down for a few minutes, she might be able to sneak out to the courtyard. She knew the palace better than he did. She could stay away from him, hopefully for enough time for the assassin to find her and try to poison her again. If she could draw the assassin out, Devin would be able to find out who was doing it, and stop it before the other sidhe arrived.

Nessa paced again, thinking of how to exactly go about distracting Devin, and ended up in her bedroom. When the door to her apartment opened, she rushed back out just as Devin and Turner entered.

"You can use the room over there," Devin said, directing Turner to the second, and empty, guest room.

"Did you find anything?" Nessa asked before Turner could leave.

"Yeah, when they depict fairies in movies and books with fairy dust, I know where they got that from. You guys dust everything with your sidhe magic, and it stinks," Turner replied and added two sneezes to emphasize his reaction to the magic. "I couldn't get a clean scent off of a single body. They were too covered in fairy dust."

Nessa had very little time in the outside world to know what Turner was talking about, but Devin was grinning; therefore, he understood and probably agreed completely with him. She was unsure if it was an insult or compliment, but let Turner walk away without asking more, even though she didn't understand.

"How is Ronan?" Devin asked as Turner shut the door to the room and headed off to the bathroom.

"Sleeping," Nessa replied, still unsure if fairy dust was a bad or good description.

Devin looked into the first guest room and could see Ronan on the bed. He nodded, and Nessa couldn't help but smile. Devin sincerely cared about her family. He could be a bit of an overprotective pain, but Nessa counted him as family. That much would never change.

"And you?" Devin asked, turning back to her.

"Me?" Nessa asked, confused.

"How are you doing with all of this?" Devin took her hand and pulled her toward their bedroom.

"What do you mean?" Nessa asked. She was confused by the worry that was dripping off him.

Devin shut the bedroom door behind them and led her to the bed. After he sat down, he pulled her on to his lap. Nessa's heart beat faster. They had not had more than a couple of moments alone since they'd arrived in the sidhe village, and most of those moments were spent sleeping or fighting. Besides, Devin wasn't one to easily show emotions.

Devin's hands slid up her arms.

"You are planning something dangerous," he replied.

Nessa yanked her arms out of his grasp and slid off his lap. He had been reading her thoughts. She made sure not to peek into his, but he didn't seem to have the same respect. Devin quickly grabbed her hands before she could stand and move further away, essentially keeping her next to him.

"I wasn't looking into your mind," Devin added, knowing exactly what to say.

"Then how'd you know that was what I was just thinking?" Nessa asked, calling him on his ability to counter exactly what she had thought.

"I don't need to look into your mind when you react like that. You seem to think I need the bond to know you, but I don't. I have been watching you for over a month now. You are the one mystery I feel like I can never unravel, but I keep watching and remembering every single thing you do. You are magical, and you entrance me. I need to know more, need to know exactly what you think … need you," he added, begging her with his eyes to not be mad.

Nessa couldn't remain angry at him because Devin was one of the most honest people she knew, but it was hard for her. The sidhe lived their lives based on lies—they changed their appearance, played word games, and never told the truth—but Devin was the exact opposite. He was completely open and honest with her.

"I didn't go into your mind before, but when you get really excited, feelings and thoughts drift across the bond. I can't help but see that you were planning something," Devin explained. "I'd never go looking around your mind without your permission. I respect you far too much for that."

Nessa pouted, but she wasn't really mad. Devin knew that, but she kept her pout up anyways.

"I wasn't planning anything. I was coming up with options," Nessa replied. "We need to find this person, or people, quickly. Sidhe will be arriving tomorrow, and we can't have any accidents or it will be war. We also can't postpone or Maureen will have time to get everyone on her side about Fiona. This is a no win situation, but I feel like the coronation has to proceed."

"I know." Devin pulled her close to him.

"I just figured if I was out of my bubble, seemingly unprotected, the assassin would show. They tried once and didn't kill me. I'd make a good target. And before you suggest someone else like my uncle, don't. I can't ask anyone to risk being poisoned. I know what it feels like, and I survived," Nessa told Devin. It was nice to have him close by. He had been running around a lot in the past two days.

"I wouldn't suggest your uncle. I don't think he has anything to worry about," Devin replied.

"There's an assassin running around that tried to kill two of his kids. He shouldn't worry about himself now that they're

131

safe?" Nessa replied. It seemed like she was missing something big as Devin calmly explained his thoughts to her.

Devin smiled. Nessa saw in his eyes what she felt. She had found her partner in life. They were on the same page, even if she didn't get what Devin was saying at the moment. He cared about her, and he cared about the sidhe. Her grandfather was right in giving Devin the power to protect everyone. He would make a great king for the sidhe, and would probably the best they ever had.

"No. I think he's completely safe. I am pretty sure only the younger generations have to worry about this particular assassin," Devin replied. "When we went back to see the bodies, I finally saw the pattern we'd missed thus far. Old Bray was the only one over the age of thirty in the tombs, and he was accidentally poisoned with the food meant for Owen. He wasn't the target. Someone is targeting the next generation of sidhe. Somehow, the entire next generation is who is being killed. I don't know why, but that's what I think is happening."

"We know who to keep track of then, right? There aren't many left of my generation in the head families. There were less than a couple dozen to begin with, and now, after everything, there can't be a lot left. The assassin has killed how many so far? Three, four?"

"Six," Devin answered. Nessa stared at him in shock. She hadn't heard of the others. "I don't know when or how, but there were two more laid out with the others when we were down there. They were both young, and not dead long."

"Then that should be good for us to find the assassins. We just need to stay with the younger sidhe of each family, and keep track of them. How many people do we have to keep track of that are not within the walls of my room, or their own, recovering?" Nessa calculated everything out. They needed to find this person, or people, and they had to do so now.

"Three, and that's the problem. I can watch one and Turner can watch one, but there is no one else to watch the third," Devin answered. "Sean is the last of the Miller youth, five-year-old Tara is the last O'Ryan, and Fiona is the last Ferguson."

"Didn't the Miller and the O'Ryan families already lose someone?" Nessa asked. Devin nodded. "And the Ferguson family is the only one who hasn't lost a person?"

"Correct."

"Would it be safe to assume that might be planned? Could Maureen be in on it?" Nessa asked. She was beginning to hate Maureen more than she already did, and that was saying a lot; even if Maureen was the last person alive, Nessa wouldn't help her survive.

"I assumed that Maureen was behind it when you were one of the first ones attacked. She's not about to give up the chance for power," Devin replied. "I've seen, and dealt with, many like her. They don't back down, and are willing to risk everything, including losing their family name. She's so set on power that she can't see how it hurts her family."

"Then it's simple. You follow Tara, and Turner follows Sean. The assassin is bound to attack one or the other. Then we can find out who it is," Nessa replied. She still didn't like putting other people out there to be hurt, but Devin wouldn't even consider allowing her to be the target.

"And we hope that it wasn't a coincidence that Fiona hasn't been touched yet," Devin replied. He leaned in and kissed her gently before standing. It was time to catch the assassin. He wanted to stay and spend more time with Nessa since they'd had so little together as it was, but they had no choice. This had to be done now.

Nessa didn't hear any doubt in his voice, but she still felt a bit uneasy. It really could have just been a fluke and the assassin is unrelated to Maureen. To top it off, Fiona was pregnant. Could she withstand the poison if it came to that? Was she really in on it? Or what if it were just a coincidence? Were they risking Fiona and her child's life by not taking her into account? Nessa hoped not.

CHAPTER 9

Devin walked away, leaving Turner with the fifteen-year-old Sean Miller. The Miller family wasn't too happy to see Devin, or hear his offer—rather order—but they weren't about to tell him no. They were scared, as they should be; Sean was the last youth in their family. Without him, they would have to choose a new main family to send to the palace to represent them. For most of the sidhe, that meant family infighting, and possibly more deaths. Devin was never going to understand the elite sidhe. How could you kill one of your own? The Millers were as headstrong as the rest, and resented Devin, but they also knew that he was protecting Nessa. They couldn't deny how well-trained he was, even if he was not a full sidhe.

Devin stopped by the kitchen, needing to be sure the food was fine since preparations had already started for the new sidhe to arrive. Any trace of poison had to be gone. He tried his best to stop by before every meal since the cook still swore she had no idea how the poison had gotten in the food.

Devin moved from dish to dish of food, and loaf to loaf of bread, from the main dishes to the desserts. Everything already prepared was fine. He then moved on to check the supplies in the adjoining room. Everything had to be looked over, had to be safe. Devin picked up lids on barrels of supplies and looked inside.

"Not being fed well enough?" someone asked from the doorway.

Devin turned and smiled. The castoff Colin was leaning across the doorframe.

"No. Fed quite well, actually. Much better than they allow you guys," Devin replied. That much was true.

Colin nodded in agreement. "I figured since I've never seen you in the village you had to be here in the palace. Must be dreadful."

"Mmm." Devin shrugged. He wasn't about to say that the elite sidhe were bad, no matter what he thought of them. Nessa had faith, and he had to believe that maybe there were a few good ones in the bunch. Gemma and Ronan seemed to shine brightly in the dark world of the elite. There had to be others. "Quite a bit different than I'm used to."

"I'd guess that. I remember as a child being told of the outside world. It sounded scary until I was a castoff. Now it sounds a bit inviting … if I could leave, of course," Colin replied.

"You can't leave?" Devin asked. They were reclusive, but he didn't know that they couldn't leave. He just thought the sidhe chose not to, especially after seeing Nessa's reaction to the outside world. She just about curled up in the fetal position when they stopped for gas on their drive to the mountains from his original home.

"Castoffs are actually treated much like day humans. Neither of us can leave," Colin replied. "Kind of goes with being different. They like to keep you around to make themselves feel better."

Devin nodded. That may have been the rule, but it didn't apply to him. All he needed was a tree, and he could be gone as easily as the other sidhe. Actually, he didn't think it even applied to him days ago. Nessa would have never brought him into the village if she didn't know a way out. Maybe he would have to look into that for Colin as well. But why couldn't Colin just leave? What was stopping him?

"The trees?" Devin asked. *Why didn't Colin just touch a tree and leave?*

"You must not get it. I can't physically leave because they can restrict the trees," Colin replied. He rolled up his sleeve to show a raised circular scar on his arm. "This makes it so that I can't leave. It makes me a castoff."

Slowly, Devin stepped closer in the dim light and looked at the mark. It was over two inches in diameter, and had some scratching in the middle. He was sure if he searched his new memories that he would be able to interpret what it meant. Backing up, he looked closer at Colin. It wasn't the only scar on the young man. His body was riddled with marks, from his exposed arms to the spots around his middle that showed through his tattered clothing. He was young, as Devin could see by his face, but his body was much older. Devin wondered what kind of life he had lived. It wasn't what a normal teenager would have been through, that was for sure.

"You know the rules," a deep, angry voice said behind Colin. Devin moved, throwing up his arm and catching the whip as it came down to strike Colin's ragged back. That accounted for some of the scars.

"Rules?" Devin asked, getting angry at the treatment of the young sidhe, who was doing nothing wrong.

The cook immediately began to tremble and stared only at the ground once she noticed Devin.

"Sorry, sir," the cook blubbered, her face red and sweating profusely. "I thought the urchin was trying to steal food again. I've caught him twice now taking palace food." The cook was trying to explain her actions, but it made no difference to Devin. There was no reason to strike Colin, who was obviously relaxing in the doorway.

"He wasn't trying to take anything," Devin replied. "He was merely talking to me."

"Please forgive me," the cook replied, slowly backing away.

Devin shook his head in disbelief. No wonder Colin had many scars. Devin shooed the cook away, and she ran back into the hot kitchen, blending into the working staff as quickly as she could. Devin hadn't meant to be mean, but the action of the cook was uncalled for, even if Colin had been caught stealing before. He clearly was not doing anything wrong now.

Colin whistled. "You must be the pet of someone very powerful to have that effect."

Devin shrugged. He had given up trying to convince the sidhe he wasn't a pet. Those in the palace knew him, and knew that he wasn't just a toy of Nessa's, but everyone else was still clueless. It was inconceivable to them that a day human could be walking around on his own. It was just one more thing he would have to change in the sidhe world. They needed to be more open, and they needed to see the outside world.

"Do you need anything?" Devin asked, waving his arms around to include the room.

Colin's eyes grew large. "And have the cook never allow me to return? No thanks."

"She seems to have let you return thus far even though you've been caught twice now …" Devin looked around the room. There had to be food in storage that Colin needed. Their tiny lean-to barely had anything in it.

Colin grinned mischievously. "The last time I kind of had way more than I should have. I was trying to take back for all of the castoffs. Guess I should have stuck to taking just a little bit."

Devin understood completely. It would be hard to return there with food and supplies to see that your neighbors have nothing. He would have done the exact same if he were in the position. Devin looked at the grinning young man, and realized his life could have been just like that if Lord Randolph hadn't taken him in. He'd had no family left after they were murdered when he was a child. No one would have raised him. He would have never lived a life of privilege. It would have been different. Even now he was lucky he fell in love with the sidhe princess. That, too, gave him power and luxury that he didn't really earn. If Nessa was anyone else, it could have been him and Nessa living in those conditions.

Colin looked behind him, and then back at Devin.

"I better get going. The cook may listen to you now, but I don't want to be around when she changes her mind. Thanks for standing up to her, and thanks for the milk. Mara was overly happy when I got home to show me what you did," Colin told Devin, still looking around the kitchen. "I'm glad you didn't get in trouble."

"Not a problem," Devin replied. "I hope I can help more when I get time. Right now things are a bit busy around here."

"The coronation, yeah, heard about that. Probably the reason the cook hasn't beat me to death yet. She needs the fruit I find, and the flowers Mara grows. Nice that we have useable talents unlike some of the others," Colin added, making his way through the kitchen. Devin followed behind.

Colin turned, heading in the opposite direction that Devin was going, and Devin watched the young man walk away. The castoffs were going to be a priority once all of the dust was settled with the assassins and the coronation. They deserved better.

Walking through the hallways, Devin searched for the child Tara. His ability told him exactly where to go, but he wasn't expecting to find her behind a desk. He had made it to the only school in the palace. Tara sat near the back with only four other children in the room. They were all older than her, and none were from head families. When Devin walked into the room, the teacher stopped teaching. Devin nodded for her to continue, and she reluctantly did so as he sat down and looked around. The children all turned to stare at him, and he felt bad for disrupting the class. However, when he didn't reply, they turned back to the teacher.

The room was like most schools. There were several desks pointed to the front of the room, though most were unfilled. The students sat, trying to watch the teacher at the front of the room, but now she was having an even harder time keeping them from distraction while the kids took turns turning around to catch glimpses of Devin. He ignored them and surveyed the room. There was no one around, but he needed to be sure that they were safe. Two windows on the opposite wall faced into the courtyards outside the school. Devin scanned the outside for anyone that could be lurking. It seemed safe, but he couldn't let his guard down.

The lesson continued and Devin grew bored with the talking. He allowed his mind to wander as he kept guard over the young child. He had to stay diligent, but he didn't have to relearn lessons he had long forgotten.

Who had the most to gain by the head families losing all of their children? So far only the Ferguson family was untouched, which meant it was probable that they were responsible for the killings. If there was no direct line to contest, they would automatically be next in line to the throne. However, it could, while slim, be that Fiona had not been touched yet as they were the only head family left with one direct heir. Who would that leave to win if everyone loses? Could the elite that were not part of the head family be responsible for killing their own? Would they even do that? Devin had no clue. Could the commoners be responsible? Devin had wandered the streets.

Most of the commoners didn't even care about the elite in any way. In fact, none of them actually even talked about the elites. They lived in their own little world. That left either the Fergusons or the other elites.

'Nessa, what happens to a head family when all of their direct descendants are killed off?' Devin asked across the bond.

'If there's no one related back one generation, to the grandfather or grandmother, then they get to choose a new head family from their own elite in their village,' she replied.

'Then if one family wanted more power, they just kill off their relatives?' Devin asked. It would be easy to do. Each elite family had their own wing of the palace, and they would be easy targets for each other across, or within, families.

Nessa understood the logistics Devin was thinking of through the bond. *'No, the new family must come from the village. Anyone living here in the palace would move back to their own family village.'*

Then it was not elites killing off their own families. That was a bit of a relief. He didn't want it to be that complicated, as he would never find an answer there. If they lost their head family, they would all be downgraded to outside of the palace. That was one more crossed off his list. But that didn't mean it couldn't still be the elite, just not the elite within the walls of the palace.

'Is it a crime to kill off your own family line?' Devin asked. Sidhe rules were all a bit skewed, if you asked him.

'It's a crime to kill anyone, if you get caught, or if you could prove someone killed your family,' Nessa replied.

That was not what Devin was expecting to hear. The sidhe were constantly killing each other. If it was a crime, why would they continue? How come no one was ever caught or punished.

'Is your system of justice skewed here?' That had to be the answer Devin was looking for.

'Justice system? No, that's fine, but our investigations lack a little, if you didn't notice,' Nessa replied.

That Devin had noticed. Lacking wasn't the best word to describe it. It was non-existent, which was why he had gone to Mori. He needed to know more, and they didn't have the ability to help him in the village. There was one more thing for him to add to his list of changes. That list was sure growing larger each day!

'Thanks,' Devin replied as he looked back outside the windows. A couple of young sidhe passed on their way to whatever house they worked for.

If it wasn't the common sidhe, it was more than likely Maureen. Yet, if it wasn't Maureen, was it likely the outside sidhe were responsible? Would they plan it together? Devin was pretty sure all of the villages were remote and isolated, but would they work together to change the palace? It would be a great master plan. Kill off all of the existing ruling sidhe, and then they could all take over at one time. Were the sidhe really like that? The more he considered it, the more it began to make sense. Who had more of a motive to kill, Maureen or the families? Maureen wanted to be queen herself. She had motive to kill Nessa and her cousins, but she didn't need to wipe out more than that. Whoever was killing off the sidhe was doing it to kill off all of the families. Maureen was becoming less suspicious … even though Devin kind of wanted it to be someone who wasn't the littlest bit remorseful about sending her son to kill Nessa.

Devin glanced back to the window and saw shadows of people that he couldn't make out. Tara was sitting near one of the windows, far too exposed for Devin's taste now that he was even more certain she was a target. She was just a young child. Devin didn't want her in on the war. In order to change the elite, he would have to start with the children, young ones like

Tara. She didn't need to be a target. Devin would find another way. He stood abruptly and walked over to the child who, like the others, was distracted.

"Would you like to have a tea party with Princess Vanessa?" Devin asked the young child.

Her eyes lit up at the suggestion, and she vehemently nodded.

"Sounds good." Devin offered the child his hand. Smiling, she took it without fear, which was a nice change for him.

The teacher stopped mid-sentence and stared at Devin.

"Tell her parents that she is visiting the princess. I'll return her by bedtime." Devin wanted to add *maybe*, but he wasn't about to tell that to the parents or the teacher. They needed to move into the protected room, and they needed to go now. Tara was not going to be one more body in the crypt.

Devin looked at Nessa and Tara sitting together at Nessa's kitchen table. Nessa wasn't a tea drinking type of girl, but she was playing right along to keep Tara entertained. It didn't seem to matter if Nessa was good at pretending or not. Tara seemed completely enamored with the future queen.

'I need to go back to my car and cell phone. Mori should be calling soon,' Devin told Nessa, and smiled at her from across the room. She looked comfortable with the young sidhe. She had a knack for engaging the girl.

Nessa gave him a *what* look in reply to his stare.

'I never really pictured you as the mothering type, but it seems maybe you're a kid person after all,' Devin added as he stood. He began to walk out of the room before Nessa could respond. He was only teasing, but he didn't want to anger her again, since she had seemed to forgive him for being overprotective.

"Mr. Day Human," Tara called. The little girl stood up and ran from the table, catching Devin in a hug. "Thanks for taking me to this great tea party. I've never met a real princess before. She's much better than my mother tells me."

Smiling, Devin patted the young child's head as she kept her arms around Devin. He wasn't exactly a kid person.

"And you're not too bad, either. They say all sorts of stuff about you, but now I see none of it is true. I kind of like you, Mr. Day Human." The little girl finally let go of Devin and hurried back to Nessa at the table.

'Yes, Mr. Day Human. You're not too scary,' Nessa mocked as he walked away.

Devin decided with Turner watching Sean, it was safe enough for him to take a hike through the woods to his car instead of using the trees for immediate transport. He had energy to waste after sitting around watching Tara for part of the morning, and running always made him think better. He took off through the woods, feeling the air whip past him as he ran. His new sidhe power gave him an advantage as he jumped over obstacles and ducked with greater efficiently than he ever had before. Life as a kind-of-sidhe wasn't as bad as he'd first thought.

His car sat in the parking lot when Devin arrived. He almost felt bad that she was just sitting there, collecting dust. He never went long without his car. It was all he had that he truly felt was his ... that he'd called his own. He had rebuilt the entire car on his own, using money he'd earned at odd jobs when Lord Randolph allowed him to work. He could have easily asked his guardian for a car, and it wouldn't have been a problem to choose the most expensive one out there, but Devin wanted to build his own.

Devin opened his car and quickly grabbed his phone. There was a missed call from Mori. He dialed him back and waited for the techie dearg-dul to answer.

"Finally made it back to civilization?" Mori asked.

Devin replied with a question, "Did you find out what it is?"

"Yeah, yeah," Mori added, dragging out the conversation. "It is a bit strange. We found that it is Tolocandies."

Devin shook his head. Sometimes, it could be a bit difficult dealing with Mori. He was extremely bright, but often forgot that not everyone else spent as much time in the lab and on computers as he did. Devin had no clue what that word even meant, let alone why it was strange.

"And that means what?" Devin asked.

"It's an extinct plant," Mori replied. "As in, why did you bring me a poison from a plant that has been dead for at least thirty years?"

"Extinct?"

"Yes, extinct," Mori replied.

"As in the way animals can go extinct?" Devin tried to clarify. He really hadn't heard of a plant becoming extinct before.

Mori gave a long-winded explanation, "Yes, and plants can go extinct, too. You hear about animals more than plants, but it can happen to plants as well. Most of the time things die out by accident, over poaching and all that, but this one was man-made. It's a very powerful toxin. The sidhe had been cultivating and growing it for centuries. They can make several different poisons from different parts of the plant, but they realized that it was a double-edged sword. While it was great to use on their enemies, when they turned to using it on each other, it was outlawed. Nessa's grandfather led the last harvest, and killed off all of the remaining plants they could find about thirty years ago."

"So it's extinct?" Devin reiterated. How could a poison be made from a plant that was considered long dead? Did someone manage to hold on to some of the poison longer than

Devin had been alive? "Someone kept it around?" Devin asked.

"I really doubt it. I heard there were people involved in the hunt for the plants that could feel difference between plants. They knew exactly where to look for each one. When they did the hunt, Nessa's grandfather led it to make sure the sidhe would be safe. It really should be extinct. I have no idea how you got a poison that has been gone for thirty years," Mori replied.

That was a good question. If there were no plants, then where did the poison come from?

"Could someone have saved the poison?" Devin asked, trying to cover all options. He didn't doubt that Mori had the correct poison, even if it seemed impossible. Devin trusted Mori's analytical abilities completely.

"That's the strange part. The poison loses its effectiveness within twenty-four hours of the leaves being picked. Someone had to be growing the plant for this poison to be around and useful. You were lucky you brought them to me when you did. Even the samples were quickly degrading. We were barely able to make out the poison in the first few samples."

"How do we counter it?" Devin asked. He needed a cure to it that could be administered when he didn't get there quick enough.

"There is none. It kills everyone," Mori replied.

That changed the game, and wasn't what Devin wanted to hear. It was bad enough the poison acted fast and was hard to catch, but to hear it degraded just as quickly was a problem. Turner was going to have a hard time tracking anything if it was gone as quickly as it killed. If they didn't find it, more people would die.

"Someone had to be growing the plant, but how is beyond me," Mori added. "I swear, all records say that every single plant was killed off."

"How do I find it?" Devin asked. Now it was time to go hunting. Devin was unsure how you looked for one plant in a world full of them, but he had to do it … and he had to succeed.

"I sent a text with a pic for you to see," Mori replied. "It's old, and black and white, but you should get the main idea of the shape of the leaves and flowers. It grows as a small shrub. They take about five years or more to mature. The leaves are almost heart shape, and it makes a small, white flower. When you do find the plant, be careful. Don't try to pull it out, or cut it down. It's very resilient. Just burn it, wherever it is."

Devin nodded to himself. That would be the plan, if he could find it.

CHAPTER 10

Devin walked back into Nessa's room, already forming his next plan. Inside, Turner was waiting, along with Tara and Sean. Devin didn't have time to explain to the two of them the importance of staying with Nessa in her room. He'd just automatically made the spell surrounding the room include the two kids. He had no clue how it came to him, but stress seemed to amplify his ability. Only Turner, Devin, and Rolf could come and go as they pleased. Nessa jumped up as Devin entered, and followed him back into her bedroom. Tara and Sean, who were playing some sort of board game at the table, didn't even seem to notice.

"Did Mori find out what it is?" Nessa asked in hushed tones so that the two in the front room wouldn't hear. It was clear that they didn't know what was happening.

"Yeah. An extinct plant made into a poison," Devin answered. "I guess your grandfather was involved in getting rid of it. It's very powerful, and there's no cure."

Nessa's mouth hung open. "Deadheart weed? Tolo something or another."

"So you know what it is then?" Devin asked. She might have suggested it before.

"Of course I do—everyone does—but it's impossible. That can't be what it is. Mori had to get it wrong," she added. "My grandfather worked with a team to get rid of all of it. They destroyed every plant that was growing in the villages, and every plant that was growing wild around here. He was sure they were all gone."

"Well, not everything was gone. Maybe someone found a way to conceal it," Turner suggested. He had faith that Mori was right.

"You can't conceal it from a plant seeker," Nessa replied. She was confused by the results of the analysis. "They feel the plants and know where each and every one is. My grandfather's first ability was to seek out plants. He could tell, for miles, what plant was where. My family is very connected to plants, and his power was stronger than normal. No one could have hid a plant from him."

Turner's eyes bounced between Nessa and Devin. She was looking at him, waiting for him to reply.

"Not something I've learned yet," Devin finally replied. It would have been useful to know this earlier, but everything having to do with the sidhe was a learning curve. He needed to see it be done, or be stressed to do magic he had no clue about. Even if Nessa had told him that there was a chance, he wouldn't know how to do it. Devin wished the old man's powers came with an instruction manual.

"He should be able to do it, right?" Turner asked Nessa, getting what she was hinting at.

"He should be able to do everything my grandfather could do. I know Devin can once he learns how, but since he was not born a McKinny sidhe, he must have to figure it all out." Nessa sounded disappointed, and Devin hated to hear the defeat in her voice. She smiled at him, and it made it seem not quite as bad. She wasn't mad at him, or even sad, she just didn't like the situation. Devin had a feeling it made her miss her grandfather a bit more. She wasn't the one who'd spoken with the old man days ago; in fact, she barely got to see him before he disappeared into dust.

"But that's fine since I have a friend with an excellent sense of smell," Devin replied. He had to be two steps ahead. He had magic now, but didn't know how to use it, so he had to be willing to use good old detective skills to get things done. "I figure it will take time, but my puppy and I can go wing to wing in the palace first, and then to each compound, searching for plants, especially hidden ones. Mori sent me a picture of what it looks like. Once Turner finds it, I can see if it's what we are looking for."

Turner glared at him. Devin knew Turner hated to be called a puppy, and that was the exact reason he did that. Nessa shook her head at their play fighting. Neither was serious about the insults, and they both knew it.

"Just be careful," Nessa replied. "It's really poisonous."

"Yeah," Devin nodded, "Mori explained that we must burn it to get rid of it." Devin nodded to Turner and they both walked out of the bedroom, toward the front doorway.

Once again Nessa hurried over, stopping Devin by grabbing his hand. When he turned to see what more she needed, she gave him a quick kiss before letting him go. It almost seemed like this was becoming a ritual for them. Tara giggled and Sean whistled as they watched. Devin tried to hide his smile as he turned to the two remaining sidhe children.

"Don't leave this room. It isn't safe out there. In here, Nessa will protect you," Devin told them. Sean pouted a little and tried to puff out his chest to make himself seem more impressive. "If you are really nice, I bet she could show you a few new fighting moves." Sean brightened at that thought.

Turner waited in the hallway for Devin to finally leave the room. "Where to, boss?"

"Let's go make a short trip outside of the palace first.

There's someone that grows plants really well that I want to ask some questions," Devin replied, not fully explaining himself. Luckily, Turner didn't ask more. They had been friends for a long time, so Turner trusted Devin, and his judgment, completely.

Devin led the way through the village to the outskirts. It wasn't hard to find his way now after wandering around a couple times. Devin had already mapped out the whole village in his head. He stopped at the first run-down house as they entered the castoff's encampment. Devin paused at a partial fence that needed a few more pieces to be complete. Mara was in the garden, on her hands and knees, talking to a plant. Turner raised his eyebrows at Devin as if to ask what was going on, but Devin just shook his head. They waited a few moments and watched as a plant sprouted out of the ground. It grew, becoming full size in less than a minute.

"Hello, Mara," Devin called from outside of the fence. The young girl looked startled, but stood and smiled at Devin.

"Day human. You've returned for a second time today?" she teased, wiping her dirty hands on her newly cleaned skirt. She looked better than the last time he had seen her in the morning, and he was sure that the milk had done some good for the young woman.

"I had some plant questions," Devin replied. "I'm looking into something for my girlfriend."

"What?" she replied with a chuckle. "You sound serious. Were you a detective in the day human world?"

"Something like that," Turner mumbled for Devin to hear only. "More like prodigal child."

"No, not a detective. Just trying to find some answers." Devin nodded to Turner. "This is my friend, Turner. He's a night human, too. He's here to help me. We need to know more about the plants around here." Mara looked Turner over with the same expression everyone in the village wore when they were walking around.

"First a day human in love with a sidhe, and now a new night human in the village. This must be some sort of crazy week," Mara replied. She didn't just look better, her spirits were up, too. Devin was finally seeing some of the youthfulness return to the young woman. "So what did you need to know?" She waved them into her garden to sit on the broken-down benches she had in the middle of the foliage.

Devin sat across from Mara, but Turner remained standing. He was still taking in the surroundings, and was a bit on guard. There was no threat to either Turner or Devin, but Devin was sure that Turner had talked to Nessa, and promised to keep him safe. It was funny to think he needed to be kept safe, but Devin knew the feeling. It was why he didn't allow Nessa out of her room. They both had the same idea: they wanted the other safe at all times.

"How many people have plant abilities like you do in this village?" Devin asked. They needed to know where to look for the assassin.

"Plant abilities are fairly rare, except for the McKinny clan," Mara replied, brushing her hands over the flowers next to her. They responded by straightening up and blooming a bit bigger for her. "All of the others maybe have one or two plant people."

Devin already knew that most of the McKinny clan was associated with plant magic, but there was no one left to investigate there. Ronan and Gemma were both poisoned, and Rolf wasn't about to do anything to his children or niece. There might have been more to worry about in the McKinny village, but Devin, for some reason, didn't think it was them.

"So your family isn't based on plants?"

Mara laughed. "Gosh, no. They were excited when I

showed plant abilities, but when they never grew past flowers, they were ready to marry me off. They'd had high hopes for me, but what can you do? You don't get to choose your ability."

"What more would they want?" Turner asked. He didn't know exactly what her ability was, but it was strange that any ability that rare would be brushed off.

"They wanted me to be able to grow trees, or something a bit more substantial," Mara replied. "They wanted what I couldn't do."

"She can make flowers grow from seed, but nothing bigger," Devin told Turner. Turner didn't see a difference, but nodded, and let them continue talking.

"Does anyone have a plant seeking ability right now, like the former king?" Devin asked. He needed a teacher, and quickly. He didn't care what clan they came from. If necessary, he could always frighten one into teaching him.

"No, not at this time," Mara replied, finding the questions odd but not commenting on it. "He was pretty unique, though. Maybe in the McKinny village there's one, but none here."

Devin nodded and thought for a moment. If there was no one to teach him, he and Turner would have a harder time hunting for the poison. They would have to rely completely on Turner's ability to sense dirt. Yet even that would be hard, because most of the houses had dirt floors. They had a long day ahead of them.

"Would you mind if we walked around your garden and house to get a better idea of the difference between planted plants and the earth that is used when making homes?" Devin asked. Mara gave him a look like she thought he was out of his mind, but nodded yes. She didn't know what type of night human Turner was, but it was about to become clear.

Devin stood. "How great of a difference between the dirt do you need to smell? Will this work?"

Turner shrugged. Dirt was dirt to Devin, but he knew better than to think Turner smelt the same. Having a lycan for a best friend was coming in handy. Turner walked into the ramshackle house and took a whiff. Then he came back outside and took another whiff. He shrugged at Devin while Mara watched in wonder.

"That should be enough. I should at least be able to tell if someone if growing a plant in their place. We'll have to search for it then, but we will know which rooms to search," Turner explained.

"What?" Mara asked, still watching Turner intently.

"He's a lycan," Devin replied, which pretty much explained it all, and Mara seemed to understand what it meant

Devin hoped Turner's abilities would be enough to save them. Time was running out. Devin made his way out of the garden and Turner followed, still looking around like someone might attack.

"Thanks," Devin called back to Mara. She nodded as they turned to leave. They'd walked a few feet before Devin thought of another question.

"And the Ferguson family here in the village … do they currently have a plant magic person?" Devin asked. That was the real truth behind it. If they did, it would be the first person they would need to visit.

"Not right now," Mara replied. "They exiled their last one years ago."

That made everything even more complicated. Devin was sure that Maureen was involved somehow, but if she didn't have anyone to order to grow plants, and couldn't do it herself, then could it really be her? Did she bring someone in from the other villages? Was it not Maureen at all? Devin didn't think that was possible. No one in the Ferguson family had been killed, and that could be a coincidence, but Devin doubted that. How was Maureen doing it, then? Was she working with outside help? Devin was sure that no one had entered the village that wasn't part of it—he would have felt their arrival— but what if someone had already been hidden inside of the village before he got his sidhe powers? There were too many questions to answer. They needed to first be sure the palace was poison-weed free, and then the village. After that he could block the village from people entering and exiting until he found the assassin.

Nessa impatiently waited in her room. Tara was still playing with Sean, and there was nothing Ronan and Gemma needed as they slept off the poison. She knew the risk of the assassin outside of the room, but figured the more people looking for the killer, the sooner they would be caught. Nessa opened her room doorway and tested the barrier Devin had put around it. Unfortunately, it was still there. It felt like gel to the touch, and pushed back when she pressed it. She wasn't going to get through it. She was still stuck in her room.

Nessa left her door open and scanned the hallway. Somewhere out there was the assassin, lurking and waiting to kill everyone in her room. She saw no one, but even if it was clear, he had to be there somewhere. She was sure that the assassin was watching because there was no one else for him to target. They had to move sometime. She had all day, or at least until Devin came back, hopefully with good news.

"You don't want to play?" Tara asked Nessa, sitting beside her.

"No. I want to wait for Devin," Nessa replied. "You just keep playing for me. I thought I heard that you've beaten Sean twice now." Nessa smiled at the child. She'd felt what Devin was feeling across the bond when he took her from school. Tara was completely innocent of the sidhe world. She deserved a chance to grow up and become a young lady without all of the drama going on around the elite. Devin had done the right thing by bringing the child here to protect her. The strange part was, not even her family had come looking for her. What sort of life were the young sidhe living in the palace?

"He lets me win," Tara whispered. "But don't tell him that I know. I like winning."

Tara didn't have a care in the world, and Nessa had forgotten what that was like. Even at the same age as the little girl, Nessa was already training. Tara was different. She was allowed to be a child.

"Are you worried about the day human?" Tara intuitively asked.

"Always," Nessa replied honestly. There wasn't a time he was away from her that she didn't worry, and it wasn't because of the bond.

"Because you love him?" Tara asked innocently.

Nessa scrunched up her face. Even if she were right, was Nessa about to admit that to a five-year-old?

"My mommy worries about my daddy all the time. She says it's because she loves him," Tara explained her train of thought. "I hear them talk. They say the day human is bad, but I think he must be an okay guy if he's trying to keep us safe from the assassin."

Nessa's eyes shot open. They had not told either Tara or Sean exactly why they were being held in the room. Nessa was shocked to know that Tara already knew about the assassin.

"Who told you there was an assassin?" Nessa asked.

Tara shrugged. "I heard the older kids in school talking about it. They were betting who would be killed next."

"Betting?" Nessa was stunned that they made it sound like a

game.

Nessa had thought no one was looking for the assassin because they were afraid, but it seemed that wasn't the case. No one was looking because they didn't care. Now she could understand Devin's frustration with the sidhe. What were they taught at home, if they thought you should bet on someone being killed for no reason beyond who they were? Nessa had heard Devin say hundreds of times that things needed to change, and at this moment she knew he was correct. The sidhe world needed to change.

"Am I a target?" Tara asked quietly. Her eyes were big, and she needed an answer. Nessa could tell the small child was scared, but she couldn't lie to her.

"Everyone in this room is a target," Nessa replied, pointing back at Sean and where her cousins were asleep in the next room. She didn't want to scare Tara more, but she needed to be told the truth. "And that's why we have to stay here. Devin put a protection spell on the room that won't allow the assassin or anyone else inside it but us. We are safe here. He made sure of it."

Tara nodded and stood back up. "That's why the day human is protecting us. My parents were wrong about him. He really is a great prince."

"Everyone is wrong about Devin. He's much more than just a day human," Nessa replied from her spot on the floor.

"Devin," Tara tried out the name on her lips. "I like Devin. He's a pretty good guy."

Tara hurried back to the game with Sean as Nessa kept watch outside of the room. She didn't expect Devin back soon, but she still felt the need to watch. If she caught a glimpse of the assassin, they could find him. Devin was able to link to every sidhe in the village and could recognize faces, so he would know where to find the assassin.

After sitting for at least ten minutes or more, Nessa quickly stood as someone approached. It wasn't Devin and Turner, but a female, and she was running down the hallway to Nessa's door. As she drew closer, Nessa knew who it was. Fiona stopped outside of Nessa's apartment.

"Nessa, my mother will find me soon, but I needed to talk to you without her around," Fiona explained, frantically looking behind her.

Nessa nodded warily. Fiona rarely did anything without her mother's permission, and it could easily be a trap. Nessa had once trusted the Ferguson family completely, including Fiona's younger brother, Finn, but she didn't any more. Maureen had been trying to kill Nessa for months, and Finn had even stabbed Devin to kill him just days ago. If it wasn't for her grandfather, Devin and Nessa would have both been dead. The Ferguson family wasn't one Nessa wanted to associate with, but she found herself wanting to listen to Fiona. Something was different with her.

"I want out of here," Fiona began as she continuously glanced around. The hallway was empty, and Nessa had no clue what Fiona was looking for. "I want to go into the day human world before I have the baby. I want to be free of this."

Shocked at the request, Nessa's mouth dropped open. Fiona was the last person Nessa ever expected to want out of the sidhe world. Her title might not be princess, since Nessa's brother died before Fiona could marry him, but she was basically the equivalent of one. Fiona had everything, and anything, she wanted. Her family was respected, and ran most areas of the government. Fiona could do, and could be, anything. Why would she want to leave?

Fiona looked around again. She acted like she was being watched, but there was no one there.

"Help me. For the sake of your nephew, help me. Get me

out of here," Fiona begged. Her face was strained, and worry seeped out of her. Nessa wanted to stay strong and not believe her. Since her mother had easily tricked her, Nessa had no doubt that Fiona would do the same. Fiona held out her hand for Nessa, begging with her eyes.

"I can't do anything right now," Nessa replied honestly, unsure if to trust her or not. She needed Devin around to see if Fiona was telling the truth. "Devin has locked me in this room. There's a barrier that won't allow me out or anyone else in."

Fiona looked at Nessa to see if she should believe her or not. When Nessa held up a hand and pressed on the barrier, her hand stopped just inches from Fiona's hand. Fiona pressed her hand forward and found the barrier also. They were separated by just inches. Her desperation increased and she once again glanced around frantically. She was about to have a breakdown, and looked like the wind was taken out of her sails.

"Then I'm dead," Fiona replied, and hung her head in despair. Her body shook a little as she talked. "My mother told me she just wants the baby. I'm worthless to her now. I didn't keep your brother here, and I didn't get him to marry me. She's going to have me killed for the baby." Fiona dropped her arms. She had given up.

Nessa stared at Fiona. She didn't need Devin to tell her the truth; Fiona wasn't just acting, she was actually being honest. Every fiber of Nessa's being believed Fiona, but there was nothing she could do until Devin returned. Maureen wasn't the woman she'd thought she was, but this was beyond what she could conceive any mother would do. She wanted her own daughter dead.

"Stay here," Nessa said to Fiona. "I'll tell Devin to come back. He can put you in this room, and keep you safe, too."

Fiona smiled only slightly. "Don't worry. My mother won't hurt the child." She acted like it was already decided. Fiona turned to go.

"Fiona, stay here," Nessa begged. The baby growing inside Fiona was the only family, beyond her uncle's, that Nessa had left. The baby was innocent, no matter what Rhys ever did, or even Fiona for that matter. The baby didn't deserve to be raised by Maureen. Nessa needed to help Fiona. If she wanted out of the village, Nessa had to get her out.

'Devin, come back now. Fiona is here, and begging to get away from her mother,' Nessa told Devin across their bond.

Fiona turned back to Nessa. "She'll be here soon, and neither you nor I will be able to stop her. She is evil, Nessa. Pure evil. She should be punished for all she has done, but there is no punishment that could match it."

Fiona dropped to the ground just outside of the barrier, and Nessa stared down at her. She wasn't the poised princess Nessa was used to, the Fiona she had grown up with. Her makeup wasn't perfect, her hair was falling out of its bun. Now she seemed like a normal girl ... a defeated girl. Nessa glanced up when someone entered the hallway. Fiona was right; they were coming for her. The assassin was only feet away, covered in a dark hood, and Nessa stood there watching, shocked and unable to do anything. Suddenly, Fiona hit the barrier and sprawled on the floor. Maureen, who was beside the assassin, smiled slightly at Fiona's prone body. Maureen said something to the assassin, and then began to walk from him. He bowed, and then screamed as Maureen did something Nessa couldn't make out. The assassin fled.

'Devin, get here now. The assassin was just here,' Nessa whispered across the bond. Maureen was in charge of the assassin after all.

CHAPTER 11

Devin raced through the hallways, pushing unsuspecting sidhe out of the way with either his hands or the magic he was randomly conjuring. Nessa was in trouble. The assassin was there. He needed to get to her; he needed to finally end this. The assassin had to be caught. His thoughts kept repeating as he sprinted around the bends of the palace. Turner kept up with Devin on his newly cleared pathway. He didn't hear the words Nessa spoke to Devin, but he knew only one thing would get him moving like that. They both knew how urgent it was.

Devin rounded the corner to the hallway where Nessa was still standing in her doorway. She was pressed against the boundary, staring at someone on the ground.

"Fiona's right here," Nessa shouted to him.

Devin passed Maureen as he ran to the unconscious Fiona.

"Where's the assassin?" Devin asked.

"He was beside Maureen," Nessa replied. Devin looked over his shoulder at Maureen before he knelt beside Fiona. Turner only glanced down at Fiona before standing at Devin's back, watching out for him.

'She wanted out,' Nessa told Devin silently. *'She came here to get out of the village. She was afraid her mother would kill her. Maureen showed up and so did the assassin. The assassin did*

something to Fiona, and she dropped to the ground like that.'

"I took care of him," Maureen stated as she stooped beside Devin next to her daughter. "I was too late to stop him, but was able to put a spell on him. He won't live much longer, be assured of that."

"Took care of?" Devin asked suspiciously.

"I was just out looking for Fiona. She had gone on a walk and hadn't returned. I rushed here as quickly as I could when I felt her in distress, and once I saw that man attack my child, I put a reverse spell on him. What he did to Fiona would be repaid to him," Maureen explained as if it was obvious. The matronly woman didn't even have a hair out of place, nor was she exhausted. There was no way Maureen had rushed over to Fiona.

Devin didn't look up at Nessa as she spoke more. He was too busy inspecting Fiona and keeping Maureen in his peripheral view.

'I didn't see any rushing, and if they were, it was to find Fiona before she escaped.' Nessa glared at Maureen. The lady lied perfectly, but that didn't matter anymore. Nessa couldn't say with certainty what happened with Maureen and the assassin, but she was sure they were together.

"I got the scent," Turner called from down the hallway. He had been pacing around, looking for something. "I can track him."

Devin nodded to Turner, who turned to go after the assassin. He wanted to go with him, but he couldn't leave Fiona dying. Nessa felt that through the bond, and he didn't try to hide it.

"Let me go with him," Nessa pleaded. She could help in place of Devin.

"No," Devin replied. How could he let her leave the room, even if the assassin was dying just like Fiona?

"If he was injured, he can't hurt me. Let me go with Turner," Nessa pleaded.

"No," Devin replied, inspecting Fiona for the poison. It was much more than a dart could have put into her.

"Devin, these are my people. Let me do my job. Let me keep them safe," Nessa added, putting more authority behind her voice. "I am their queen. How can I be a ruler if I hide in my room? I need to do this. Trust me to stay safe. Trust Turner to keep me safe. He will need help once he finds the assassin. He doesn't know his way around the village."

Devin finally looked up. Determination shone in her eyes. Nessa needed to go with Turner, needed to save her people. Devin understood that, and knew that he couldn't keep denying her from doing her job. She would be queen in a day. He had to let her go, no matter how much he wanted to keep her in a safe box forever. Devin sighed.

"Fine." Devin stood and took her hand, allowing her to pass through the barrier. Devin pulled her close and kissed her. "Don't do anything foolish, and keep me informed of what you find." When Devin glanced down the hallway, he nodded to Turner and knew that was enough. Turner would do everything possible to keep Nessa safe.

Nessa made a wide circle to keep away from Maureen, who sat there holding Fiona's hand. She only glanced down at Fiona, who was completely passed out. At least she wasn't feeling the pain Nessa had felt with the poison. Suddenly, Nessa could smell blood, and knew that Maureen was talking to Fiona through a blood bond—the unique way night humans could talk to each other if they connect their blood. Nessa hated to leave Fiona there, especially with her mother, but there was nothing she could do to help. Devin watched the pain cross Nessa's face, and he didn't have the heart to tell her that the poison was already too much for Fiona to survive.

Devin looked back down at Fiona as Nessa left with Turner. The poison was at least ten times the amount that Nessa had ingested before, and way more than had been in Ronan and Gemma combined. Devin made a small cut and tried the poison to see if it would pull out of Fiona. He didn't know how long it had been in her. If he were lucky, it would have just entered her, and he could get it out. It stuck to her as he suspected it would. Fiona was really in trouble.

Devin glanced at Maureen. Her expression was that of a caring mother, but her feelings—which he could slightly feel—were that of excitement. She wasn't sad at all. In fact, she was excited that her daughter was dying. Devin didn't want to deal with the lady, but needed to.

"Can she hear us?" Devin asked, knowing that they were sharing a blood bond to communicate.

"Yes," Maureen replied honestly.

Devin examined Fiona again. He had to make a plan, but what were his options? The poison filled almost each cell of her body. There was so much, he wondered how she'd even made it to Nessa to talk to her. Devin moved a little of the poison around and realized that he had two options. He could put all of the poison inside of the baby and take it out before the poison spread to Fiona, or he could put all of the poison inside of Fiona and save the baby. There was no way he could save both; there was just too much in her.

"I can save Fiona, or I can save the baby if I act now," Devin told Maureen.

"Oh," she replied, like she was shocked, but she didn't seem to mind the news at all.

"How far along is she?" Devin motioned to Fiona's protruding belly.

"The baby was due next week. It's safe to take the baby now." Maureen knew what Devin was asking. She didn't even hesitate to make it known that they should do that.

"What does she want to do?" Devin asked. He wasn't going to take the baby out if that wasn't what Fiona wanted. Without Fiona, the baby would be Maureen's to raise. That wasn't a fate he would want anyone to have, but it was ultimately Fiona's choice. It was her baby, and she was the mother.

"Save the baby," Maureen replied. Devin figured that would be the answer Maureen gave no matter what Fiona said, since she couldn't talk.

"Get a doctor here now to take the baby," Devin replied. No matter what Fiona's real answer was, the baby was going to be born now.

Maureen stood and hurried away. This time she really did look like she hurried, as her long skirt billowed behind her. Devin pricked his finger, reached down, and connected to Fiona via a blood bond.

'Do you want me to save the baby or you?' he asked her mentally.

'Save my baby,' Fiona replied.

'But if I save you, you can have more children,' Devin explained.

'But Rhys will never have more children. Save my child, Devin. Save my child from this poison. Save my child from my mother. Save my child from the sidhe world. Take him away, and don't let them ever find him,' Fiona pleaded. She'd had a complete change of heart from just days prior, and Devin was shocked to hear her words. Nessa was right. Fiona wanted out.

'Did you know your mother was using your brother to try to kill Nessa?' Devin had to ask. Why was she different now?

'No. I was mad, just like everyone else, that Rhys did not return, but when Nessa told of how he wanted to take Arianna, I felt like he got what he deserved. I never thought Nessa should be killed for it. I've known Nessa since she was a baby. She's as close

as any girl has ever been to me,' Fiona added. *'I always thought she was like a little sister.'*

'And your mother? Did you know what your mother had been up to?' Devin asked. He hated to waste more time, but he needed confirmation on his suspicions.

'No. I found the assassin meeting my mother and heard them discussing how to use the poison to kill me next. My mother knew that you suspected her. She was going to throw that off long enough to get the rest of the Ferguson clansmen in town to help her with taking over the palace,' Fiona replied. *'She's planning a war.'*

'Your entire family was going to attack?' Devin asked. This was much more than he expected. He thought they had an assassin and Maureen to deal with, but not an entire family.

'They wouldn't have a choice. My mother is the head. They have to follow her orders, or end up being castoff. They would all know the consequences if you found out or won, so they would have to stand beside her. Really, they are innocent, but wouldn't have had any other options. My mother is evil, and she's willing to do anything to have power. I never knew that meant killing me.' Fiona was hurt by everything that had happened, and Devin didn't blame her. Her own mother was having her killed by a poison with no cure. That wasn't what a mother was supposed to be like.

'And yet you still want to save the child. You know that's what she wants,' Devin told Fiona.

'I know, but I also want him to have a chance. If you save him, you can take him away. You don't have to give him to my mother. I ran away and came here because I knew you could help. You are the only person not caught in her lies. She planned to kill me back in our wing and take the baby first. This way she thinks she's going to win, but I still win. You'll do that for me, right?' Fiona was a bit worried. *'You will save my baby?'*

'I'd never let your mother have the child. This baby is innocent

of everything your family has done, and he is blood to Nessa. I will save him, and keep him from your mother,' Devin replied, looking up upon hearing footsteps rushing down the hallway. *'I will keep him safe. I promise.'*

'Thank you,' Fiona's voice drifted off as Devin let go of her hand.

Maureen returned with a portly man beside her. He was mostly out of breath, and even Maureen had a few strands of hair out of place. They *had* rushed back. Maureen reached down and took Fiona's hand again. Devin couldn't imagine what the woman was saying. Was she lying to Fiona, or gloating now that there was nothing Fiona could do about it? He hated to leave Fiona like that, but he had to do what he needed to do. His concentration had to be on saving her baby.

"Are you sure you want to save the baby?" Devin asked Maureen, giving her one last chance to care about her own child dying. "I can save your daughter."

"Fiona wants the child saved, and I have to agree," Maureen replied. "I'll do as she asks, and maybe this baby will make up for Fiona always screwing up. We have to let this baby redeem his mother for me." She glanced at the man beside her.

Screwing up? Devin wanted to ask, but pretended like he didn't hear the offhand comment made to the doctor beside her. Maureen looked down at Fiona. They were still linked through the bond, and Fiona had to be talking, which gave Devin a moment to study Fiona. The poison was flowing through her blood, and it was too much for anyone to handle. It was easy enough to get it out of the baby, but Devin needed a plan on how to get the baby within the barrier of Nessa's room as quickly as they got it out. He didn't need to promise Fiona to save the child. He would have anyway. However, he needed to figure out how to do it.

Devin studied the poison and watched as it slowly grew. He

had to make a plan before it was too late. The poison pumped through Fiona with each heartbeat. Devin put a barrier between Fiona and the baby once the deadly liquid was out of the baby and completely into Fiona, keeping the baby safe. Devin watched the poison flow. He was running out of time. One more pump, and the blood flowed from her heart and into her arms. Devin watched as it all the way into Fiona's fingers, which were touching her mother. The blood mixed a little, and Devin wished the poison was in Maureen. It would solve most of the problems. Devin suddenly had a great plan.

He needed to act quickly and be sure that Fiona completely understood his actions. He needed to be sure Fiona would not hold it against him once he did what he needed to do. Fiona had to fully back her claim that her mother was evil. It was the only way his new plan would work.

"Maureen, you can cut the pleasantries. I know that you want the baby," Devin told the older woman bluntly.

She smiled back. "Of course I want the baby. If I do it right, like I did with raising Fiona's brother, I can make certain that this one makes the family proud."

"And they are not proud of Fiona?" Devin asked. He was waiting for Maureen to call Fiona a screw-up again.

"Proud of her? The whole family would fall apart if she were left to rule it. She couldn't even get Rhys to marry her, how would she rule a family? She's an idiot that believes in love. Well, this is what you get for believing in love: a bastard child," Maureen replied bluntly. Devin sure hoped Fiona was listening. He needed to be sure that Fiona understood how bad her mother truly was. He didn't want any retribution for his newest plan.

Devin found the bond between mother and daughter, and pushed the poison toward Maureen. He hoped that his actions wouldn't come back to hurt Nessa.

"Can you make another bond to keep her strong? She's fading, and I don't know if she will survive long enough to get the baby out," Devin asked as he placed his hands on Fiona and moved the poison.

"Like this?" Maureen asked, making another cut on her second hand and grasping on to Fiona tighter. Maureen would do anything to keep the baby alive.

"So, in your eyes Fiona deserves to die?" Devin asked, starting the conversation back up as he moved the poison around.

"She should have died in place of Rhys. At least he understood how to rule. This child could have been raised by a great king if Nessa hadn't gone and killed him." Maureen was getting all of her anger out at once. Devin couldn't have asked it to go better than that. She didn't even notice as the poison entered her veins. Devin directed Maureen's clean blood back into Fiona through the second cut. He didn't know if it would work, but it seemed to be so far. They were related, after all.

"But she's your daughter," Devin added, trying to keep the conversation going.

"She's a waste of space," Maureen added. Her anger fell a little, and she wobbled with her grasp. "You can't believe how much time I have had to spend cleaning up after her. She never did anything right. I'd give her directions, and this is what I got. Seduce a king and get him to impregnate you. I didn't mean unmarried. It means nothing without a marriage. She has always been a disappointment since the first time she met Rhys. This child will never understand there's no room in marriage for love."

Devin pushed more poison into Maureen. She had to be feeling the effects, but said nothing. She was too busy complaining about Fiona. Maureen stood no chance against the poison flowing through her blood; this way, he could save

Fiona and the baby by sacrificing her mother.

"And that's why you turned to assassins?" Devin asked as the last bit of poison left Fiona.

Maureen's head snapped up, the sudden movement causing her to sit down from lack of balance due to the poison in her blood. She was falling victim to it, but coherent enough to know that Devin was trying to get a confession out of her.

"You can't honestly think I'm involved in the poison and assassinations. He attacked my daughter. I fought back against him. I have no clue who would do such a thing," Maureen added.

Devin reached down and picked up Fiona, who was still unconscious.

"I'd believe not," Devin replied as he began to walk away.

"What are you doing?" Maureen asked as she turned back toward Devin. Suddenly, she tipped over and was lying on the floor. "We need to get the baby out before the poison kills my grandson." She turned to the doctor. "I'm not feeling too well, Oran. I feel a bit sick."

"I think you should worry more about yourself," Devin added. Maureen tried to move, but her body was paralyzed. "I hear that poison is pretty quick." Devin stepped into the protected room. Ronan was standing in the doorway, watching. He easily took the sleeping Fiona from Devin and put her on the couch.

"What did you do?" Maureen asked, shaking from the pain. She really had no clue what Devin had just done.

"Well, I figured any good mother would ask for their child to be saved, and be willing to do anything to see that happen. You asked for me to save your grandchild, but not your daughter. I figured I'd give you a chance at redemption. You get to save your grandchild and your daughter now," Devin answered. "I didn't know it would work this way, but it seems if you are from the same bloodline, I can just transfer the blood between you. You take all of the poison, save your daughter and grandchild, and get to be the great mother she never had. You get to die as her savior. Isn't that great?"

Maureen opened her mouth to protest, but no sound came out. She was dying, and there was nothing anyone could do to help. Devin didn't even look back at her. He didn't care what her response was. Maureen Ferguson was an evil lady, and would be nothing but an evil lady until her last breath. Thankfully, that would be soon.

Nessa ran behind Turner, keeping close so she would not lose him. She didn't guess she'd have trouble keeping up with him, but Turner was quicker than she expected. He made very unpredictable moves as he weaved through the palace. Obviously, the person they were chasing knew the palace well, and it made Nessa wonder who it could be. There were distant cousins to Fiona that still lived in the palace, so it could be any one of them. Whoever it was, she hoped they would find them, and get answers before they died.

The path continued through the palace. Soon they were in the courtyard. The assassin was making loops as he ran back around the way he'd already come inside. Whoever this was, he didn't want to be caught, poison or no. Nessa paused as Turner approached an exit, and watched as he passed through. If she followed, the alarm would be set off. Nessa sucked in her breath and followed anyway. Squealing started as they continued to follow the pathway through the village. She didn't have time to care, or to tell anyone what she was doing. They had to find the assassin.

Turner followed on, having to pause every ten feet to confirm their direction. It was easier in the palace where there weren't as many scents. Outside there were more people and scents to confuse Turner. Nessa observed the scenery and the passing sidhe; she didn't go into the village often, and it was a lot to take in for her. The palace was well-maintained and felt not too far off from Devin's day human world. The village was much more rustic. Many of the homes were overgrown and in disrepair. People used unusual objects for doors, fences, and windows. There was no structure, or universal togetherness, from home to home. It was strange to see the disarray. Turner stopped for a fourth time and looked around.

"The assassin left the pathways here in the village," Turner explained, pointing between two houses. "It will be easier to follow him through the woods. Not as many sidhe. You kind of all smell the same, no offense," Turner added with a smile.

Nessa shook her head. How could Turner be joking at such a serious time? He didn't wait for her response, and he kept tracking. He picked up the scent and they were off into the woods. It was a slow process, even here, where he had to stop often to find the correct scent. It was good that Devin had called Turner in because he was proving invaluable. Nessa could only imagine the assassin was running full force, and right now they were taking baby steps to catch up. She hoped they could find him in time, but if the assassin knew what was best, he would be long gone before they could get him.

Turner paused and pointed over to the side of a tree. The trail turned from there. Nessa didn't have the slightest clue where they were, but she trusted Turner and his nose.

"Guess we go back into civilization," Turner said, leading the way.

Nessa followed as the path they were walking on became more pronounced. It had been used often, but Nessa had no clue why. She could sense the sidhe like Devin, just to a lesser extent. They were not near the village, yet there were a few sidhe. Why would they be outside of the village? Was this a camp of sidhe waiting to attack? Were they walking into a trap? Turner walked through two trees that provided cover. He wasn't readying for a fight, and she had to trust that, for some reason, he knew it was safe. Nessa wasn't prepared for what she saw when she passed the foliage. There was a dilapidated village before her eyes. Nessa had no clue where she even was.

Looking around, she noticed the rough, dirt pathway that meandered from home to home. It had been used and packed down, but only by human feet, not the normal traffic that walked the streets of her village. Where were they? People were outside of their homes, but most had retired for the day. Dirty faces stared at her. They wore ragged, unwashed clothing that was practically falling off each person she saw. Most were too thin, and the few remaining that were moving into the homes—if they could be called that—did so at great pains. Nessa watched an old man, who was missing a leg, as he limped with a broken crutch. They were in terrible condition, and so was their camp. How could a place like that be close to the village and no one had ever told her about it?

"Where are we?" Nessa whispered. She didn't want to call any more attention to herself than she already had. She didn't know what to make of the all the scared, sad faces staring back at her. "What city is this?"

"Yours, princess," Turner replied. He didn't know that she had never been there, but it was clear now. Nessa knew nothing of the rest of the village that was all Devin.

Turner was still following the scent. He stopped in front of a house that was hidden by a large garden. Beautiful flowers bloomed throughout the garden and grew up the sides of the rickety house. It would have been amazing except for the condition of the house. It was weathered, and Nessa could see through cracks in the walls to a dark interior. It would be in no condition to keep out the wind, or rain for that matter. Nessa had no idea how they would make it in the snow. The place looked like a good storm would knock it down. How could this be her village? Who were these people?

"This isn't mine," Nessa replied, looking around at the people. She didn't know a single face, but then again, she didn't know a single commoner in her village, either. Nessa was sure these people didn't belong to her community, as no one would be in that condition. Her people were well fed. Everyone had a job, and everyone lived happily, even if not given the same luxuries as the palace. This couldn't be her town.

"Welcome to the castoffs," Turner added, pointing to the house behind the garden. "I think you need to tell Devin to come here now. He knows these people, and he knows the assassin. I think he'll want to deal with them himself."

Nessa turned to Turner in shock. That was impossible. Devin had only been in the village for a few days. He didn't have time to meet any of the castoffs. Devin had sat on the commoner council for her, but none of the castoffs could have been there. He couldn't have known of them. Turner looked at her expectantly. He really meant for her to call Devin there. She sure hoped he was wrong. How could Devin have been there and not told her about it? She couldn't fathom her people, castoffs or not, living in conditions like this. They were starving and in need of medical help. She had no idea this side of the village even existed. Had she been that sheltered her whole life? It seemed to be the case.

'Devin, Turner said you would know where to find us in the castoff village,' Nessa told Devin mentally. *'We've tracked the assassin here, and Turner says you know him.'*

CHAPTER 12

Devin walked into the castoff camp. He made sure Fiona was poison-free before he left, and Ronan and Gemma promised to look after her. He wasn't sure he wanted to be around once she woke and found out what he'd done. The fact that she needed to get away from her mother was the most prominent feeling, but he'd also felt the love. Everything Fiona had ever done was to get her mother's affection. Devin had no clue how she was going to react when she found out what he had done, but he'd have to deal with it later. Nessa and Turner had found the assassin in the castoff camp. Devin actually considered it was a good hiding place, as most of the sidhe would never look there, but he was shocked when he found Turner waiting outside the hovel of Mara and Colin.

"We didn't go inside, but we made sure no one left. Nessa can feel two people inside, and the assassin scent ends here. I've walked around the whole house, and I'm sure the assassin didn't get out, not that there's another way," Turner reported to Devin.

Devin mentally noted that he owed Turner big time for being there and catching the assassin. Friends like Turner were hard to come by. Devin nodded to him, walked past both him and Nessa, and paused at the garden outside of the house. He looked around at all of Mara's plants, but didn't find a single bush in the mix. Mori had told him it was a bush that the poison was made from. Mara didn't have the ability to make her plants into anything but flowers—that was evident by the flowers that took over even the pathways—how could they be involved?

Devin walked up to the doorway and paused again. There was a vine growing up the side of the house toward the back where there was a tree that the walls leaned against. Devin stepped closer to look at the heart-shaped leaves. They looked very similar to the ones Mori sent, even if they weren't in the bush form. Was it possible this was the poison he was looking for? Did Mara grow that? Was it coincidence? There were no flowers, but Devin didn't get any closer just to be safe. He walked back to the door.

Devin thought back to when he'd met the pair. Mara was innocent and kind. It was hard to see her doing anything to hurt a soul. Maybe it was Colin. He was rougher on the edges, but Devin didn't feel any malice from the young man, either. Everything Colin did appeared to be for Mara. How could either of them be the assassin? Devin went over their first conversation in his head. What had he missed?

Devin knocked on the door urgently.

"Colin, open the door," he called a bit loudly to the closed door.

Nessa and Turner looked through the cracks. It was completely dark inside, but everyone could see movement within. They were in there.

"Colin, let me in to save her. I get it. Mara didn't have a choice. She is a Ferguson," Devin told the closed door.

"What?" Nessa asked, moving to stand beside Devin. Turner grabbed her arm and kept her beside him. Devin wasn't in the safest position, especially if the assassin had more poison, and Turner couldn't let Nessa get closer.

Devin turned to Turner and Nessa. "When I met them, they told me that Mara was a Ferguson. When I asked if the Ferguson family had any plant growers left, she told me no. That's because she was their last one. I swear that she wouldn't have done anything to hurt anyone unless Maureen was behind it."

Devin knocked on the door again with the same urgency. Mara was more than likely dying. She was responsible for the deaths of several elite sidhe, but that didn't matter. He needed to save her. She had been treated badly for just loving the wrong man, and Devin couldn't help but side with her. He couldn't let the idea of freedom of love die with her.

"Please, Colin, let us in," Devin pleaded to the closed door. He already knew there was magic on the door, and he wasn't going to be able to push it in easily. He was going to need to use force to enter unless he could convince them otherwise.

There was no reply. Devin sighed. How could Colin let her die?

"I promise you nothing bad will happen to either of you. I have no doubt Maureen was behind everything. Please, just let me in. Let me help," Devin pleaded. "I will keep you safe."

"What can a day human do?" Colin finally replied from behind the closed door. His voice was rough and ragged. He had been crying.

"I can do much more than you ever could imagine," Devin replied. He didn't want to show who he was to the castoffs that were now gathered and watching the scene. "Please let me in. I can show you."

The door still didn't open. The people who'd gathered around to watch began to point at Nessa. Devin heard the whispering. They knew who she was. Their voices were growing louder as each passed the message on to his neighbor. Princess Nessa was among them. Devin needed to act quickly.

177

He needed to save Mara and get Nessa back under protection. Nessa wasn't responsible for their living conditions, and had no clue about the castoffs, but they didn't know that. He didn't want any of them to turn on her right now.

In the modest hovel, a crash resounded. Devin pushed on the magic with his bare hands and felt the sting. He needed in there. Something was wrong. There was no choice. Everyone would look at him differently now. Devin let the sidhe magic race through his veins and the double swords appeared on his back. He didn't wait for a response before he pulled the blades from his back. Devin placed a sword on the corner of the door near the handle and pushed. The magic that was keeping the door shut was instantly broken by the old king's blades. After Devin sheathed the swords he reached for the handle, but stopped. He didn't need to move as the door opened from within.

Mara's big, brown eyes stared at Devin in shock. Devin was just as surprised to see her. He was sure it was Mara that was the assassin.

"You're *that* day human," she whispered as she looked at him. Devin nodded, at a loss for words. "You can help him?" she asked, pointing to Colin who was lying on the blankets in the corner of the room. It wasn't Mara after all. Colin was the assassin.

"He didn't want to help Maureen, but he did it for me," Mara told Devin as tears poured out of her eyes. "He's dying because of me."

Devin hurried over to Colin and knelt beside the young man. Devin didn't need to search his mind to know that anything he did was because he cared for Mara. Devin had just met him, but he knew that he was willing to risk anything for his love, otherwise how could he have ended up a castoff? Devin placed his hands on the young man's chest and looked for the poison in his system. He searched a second time, but there was nothing. He was poison-free. He looked just like all of the other poisoned people, but he wasn't.

"What, exactly, did Maureen do to him?" Devin asked Nessa in the doorway.

"I'm not sure," Nessa replied. She had been too far away to tell what had happened for certain. "You can communicate with any sidhe, right?" Nessa was correct. Devin now had the ability to mentally talk with any sidhe because of his new power. "Ask her?" Nessa's suggestion was logical, just no use at that point.

Devin shook his head. "Not an option."

"Why not?" Nessa asked in reply.

'Maureen is dead,' Devin replied silently since they had an audience just outside of the door.

'Dead?'

'I transferred the poison she had used on Fiona to her in order to save Fiona and her child,' Devin replied quickly. They were running out of time. It wasn't the time to have a debate about Maureen.

'Why would she poison her own daughter?' Nessa asked, but Devin didn't reply. He didn't have time for that conversation. He needed to figure out what was wrong and fix it as soon as he could.

"I can't find anything wrong with him," Devin told Mara and Nessa, hoping they could help.

"Nothing at all?" Nessa asked. Nessa figured Maureen had just used the same poison on the assassin when he howled and ran from her.

"No. There's no infection, no poison, nothing. He's completely healthy, if a bit underweight and undernourished." Devin looked back through Colin's body. There really was nothing wrong. He should have been awake.

"Could it be in his head?" Turner asked from his spot beside Nessa.

Devin looked up at Turner. He was always more the action-type of person, but that was by choice. He really could be just as perceptive and smart as anyone else; he just didn't like to show it. Devin looked back down at Colin. Turner had to be right. There was nothing that was killing Colin; it had to be in his head.

Glancing down at Colin's unconscious body, he knew what he needed to do. He had never entered anyone's head aside from Arianna and Nessa, and that was because there was a bond between him and the two girls. This was different, and somehow felt wrong, but he needed to do it to save the young man. Devin took ahold of Colin's face and closed his eyes. He used the touch to focus on the young man's mind. Devin pushed and found no barrier. Yes, it had to be all in his mind. Normal people would have fought to not let an intruder in.

Once inside Colin's mind, Devin watched the flash of images. There were childhood images of learning about his own sidhe gift. Then the images fast-forwarded to meeting Mara. They shared the same type of unique gift. They understood each other. They couldn't help but fall in love. Soon there was a wedding, and Devin watched Mara and Colin get married with their family there supporting them. They didn't have much wedded bliss before reality set in, and the images turned to the arrival of palace guards who trashed their new home and threw them into the castoff camp with only the clothing on their backs. The images returned to happy. Colin and Mara built their house on their own. They made their garden. They grew even more in love. It didn't matter where they were, they would always love each other. Devin wanted that type of love. He wanted Nessa to want him like that.

"Who's here?" Colin's voice asked from everywhere around

Devin. That was a good sign. At least Colin could still tell when someone had entered his mind. He wasn't completely gone. Devin hoped that meant he still had time to save him.

"I came," Devin replied, materializing in the blank space that was Colin's mind when the images stopped.

Colin appeared before Devin also. His hair was perfectly combed, and his clothing was no longer tattered. The man in Colin's mind was whole and had never been in the castoff camp. He looked the way he had before they went through the hardships of being in the camp. Colin's face showed shock as he stared at Devin.

"Day human?" Colin asked. "That isn't possible."

"Yes, it is me," Devin replied. "I need to know what's wrong with you. Mara is worried, and she needs you back." There was one thing that motivated Colin like nothing else: Mara.

"I can't go back to her. I was poisoned. I'm dying," Colin replied. Devin was at a loss. He needed to bring him back, and Mara wasn't even enough of a motivation. "How can you be here?" Colin was still confused by Devin's entrance into his mind.

"You aren't dying. There isn't a single thing wrong with your body. You are healthy and fine."

"You can't know that. You're only a day human." Colin wasn't mad, he was just stating what he thought was true.

"Yes. I know you're well. I checked your body personally. You're fine," Devin replied.

How was one to convince someone they were healthy when they thought they were dying? The mind was such a hard place to reconcile for Devin. Colin was a prime example. He was willing his body to die, even though it was healthy.

"Are you a doctor in your day human world? You can look over my body all you want, but you won't see the poison running through me." Colin had given up. He was ready to die.

"I'm not a doctor. I am *the* day human," Devin tried to clarify. "You know … the one that is bonded to the princess."

Colin assessed the man standing in front of him. Devin could see he was considering his options. "You mean that you're the day human prince?" Colin finally understood what Devin had meant by *the* day human.

"For now, but I suppose when Nessa is queened tomorrow that makes me the day human king," Devin replied nonchalantly. Colin just stared at him like the thought had never crossed his mind. Devin didn't appear special. No one would guess who he really was.

"That can't be," Colin replied finally, still trying to find a sliver of truth to what Devin was saying. It didn't seem possible that any day human could enter a night human's mind, so he had to be special, but Colin never saw anything of the scary leader that everyone said the day human prince was. Could it be true?

"Then how do you think I got into your mind?" Devin asked. Could Colin believe that a day human could go into random people's minds? Devin could feel some logic dawning in the night human.

That was a good argument as Colin moved closer and looked at Devin. Devin let his image include the now famous swords. Finally, Colin fell to his knees. "I'm sorry, my prince. I didn't know it was you."

Devin stared at Colin, unsure how to reply. He had yet to find someone that bowed to him for being whom he was. Devin waved off the bow, but Colin bent down so that he could only see the floor. Devin tried to get Colin to stand by pulling on his arm.

"I'm sorry I was too casual with you. Please help me leave

this world as my punishment," Colin added, face still plastered to the floor.

"What are you talking about?" Devin asked, grabbing Colin's shoulders and pulling him up. "Leave this world? I am here to bring you back to the real world. There is nothing wrong with you. And there's no reason for you to want to die."

Colin seemed to believe Devin's words now. "How can there be nothing wrong with me? I poisoned Fiona, and Maureen used the *onto you* spell. I should be suffering from the same fate as Fiona."

"Well, if that's the case, then snap out of it. You are completely fine. She's completely fine. I healed her before coming here," Devin replied. "Fiona is going to live, so shouldn't that also be your fate?"

"You couldn't have done that. The poison was too advanced to heal. You can only heal someone of that much poison in minutes. You weren't there when I poisoned her." Colin knew his poison well.

Devin shook his head. "That's one thing you sidhe need to stop saying."

"What?"

"That I can't do something. None of you can imagine the power the old man gave me. There wasn't much I could do before as a normal day human, but now it seems like there is always a way if we look for it. Yes, Fiona is fine. She is alive." Devin flashed pictures of Fiona breathing and alive as he carried her into Nessa's room for Colin.

"Then I'm not dying?" Colin asked. He was trying to grasp the situation.

"No, you are not." Devin was happy to finally have Colin understand.

"Then you need to kill me now. Don't let me wake and give Mara hope. I did it. I did it all. I killed the elite sidhe. I poisoned the food given to Princess Vanessa. Trying to assassinate the princess alone is punishable by death, but since I actually killed others my death is inevitable. I already said my good-byes to Mara. Let me go in peace now," Colin pleaded. He was back to wanting to die.

"No," Devin replied simply.

"No?"

"No," Devin said more firmly.

"But I confess. I did it," Colin replied. "I deserve to die."

"And in my world the executioner doesn't get thrown in jail when he follows orders he was given. I have a pretty good idea that Maureen was behind all of this," Devin added. He wasn't about to kill Colin for Maureen's plotting. Mara and Colin had gotten caught in her web.

Colin shrugged. "So what if she was? It's her word against mine. I'm a castoff. She's an elite. I don't stand a chance. Please, let me die now. Don't make me face her. There's nothing I can do against her."

"Who knows what she would have said, but Maureen isn't around to contradict you now," Devin added. He needed to get Colin to understand he needed to come back soon. His body wouldn't continue to function if he brain was telling it to quit.

"What?" Colin stared at Devin.

"I saved Fiona by transferring the poison to her mother," Devin replied. He didn't feel sorry for his actions. Maureen got one last chance to be a great mother.

Colin thought about that and shook his head in amazement. Devin may have power, but what made him strong was his ability to use it. Colin was glad that he was able to meet the future king of the sidhe. Devin was a good man, and worthy of the title. The sidhe needed him, and Colin wished he hadn't done as Maureen had commanded. He could have been around to see Devin change the sidhe world.

"No matter the reasons I did it, I am still guilty and nothing can take that away." Colin was set on the fact that he needed to die for his part in the poisoning.

"I don't believe in punishing someone with death if they acted on the orders of someone else without knowing all of the details. I need you to come back. I need you to stand before the sidhe and explain what you did and why. I need this to be over, and you're the key to the end. When they find that Maureen was behind everything, we will be able to move on," Devin replied. "I need you to do this for your people."

"And what becomes of me?" Colin asked. "You can't wipe clean what I've done."

"No, but I won't kill you for it. I think I can find another alternative. Just come back. Don't give up. Don't leave Mara alone," Devin threw in Mara in hopes to keep Colin alive. His heartbeat was slowing down dangerously. Even Devin was running out of time. Soon it would be unsafe for Devin to be in the sidhe's mind.

Colin looked to him and nodded. Devin sighed as he sensed Colin's body began to grow stronger. His heart beat faster, and Colin would live.

Nessa watched Devin slowly open his eyes. Colin was still lying on the ground unconscious, but his breathing had steadied. Nessa rushed over to Devin to help him stand. It took a lot to go into someone's mind, and he had been in there for over twenty minutes. Nessa would have been more worried if she didn't have the bond to peek through and see that he was okay while he was in there. Devin smiled at Nessa's gesture and stood beside her. He squeezed her shoulder under his arm. He was a bit weak.

"He's fine now. It might take a bit for him to wake. His

body was very stressed and convinced that he would die," Devin explained. He walked over to Mara and sat down in front of her. Sitting was easier than standing. "We need to know the truth, and I need to find a way to keep you two safe from the elite. You've made a lot of enemies."

"What do you mean?" Nessa asked. It was obvious that Colin had been the assassin. Why would there be retribution toward Mara?

"Mara grew the poisonous plant. Didn't you?" Colin didn't have the ability.

Mara nodded. Her eyes were filled with happy tears, but her face was masked in regret. She had not acted on her own will either, but she felt just as responsible as Colin did.

"Our families blessed our union when we married. They thought it was more than appropriate for two plant magic sidhe to marry. My father was happy to get rid of me. We kept everything pretty much a secret from the heads of our family, but everyone else around us knew. No one had a problem with it, until Maureen found out. She was horrified I would marry outside of the family and join theirs. I was the last plant person they had. The Miller family was happy with my choice, as they gained a plant person, but that didn't matter. We technically broke the rules and married outside of our families. They came and took us here, and we've been here since.

"I thought we had made it. The castoffs don't care in the least who we marry or love. We fit in here. Yes, it's hard work, and maybe a bit rundown, but we were happy." Noticing the look Nessa was giving her, Mara quickly added, "We really were happy just being together. The clans leave you alone here. You're not a Ferguson or a Miller, you're just a person. I liked it that way."

"Then when did it change?" Devin asked. Nessa could see that he cared and was really trying to find a way to help them.

"A little over a month ago, Maureen came and found us. She told me that if I didn't help her grow a plant she needed, that she was going to mark my entire family as castoffs because they technically broke the rules by not reporting Colin and me. While I was happy, I couldn't let my family be here. This is a hard life. I have little nieces and nephews that aren't even walking yet. I couldn't let this be their fate if I all I had to do was grow some plants." Mara looked over to Colin. He was peacefully sleeping now.

"So you grew the plant for her?" Devin asked. Mara nodded as she watched Colin.

"Yes, she gave me three seeds," Mara replied.

That was how Maureen was able to keep the plant away from the late king. She had her plants destroyed, but not the seeds. Who could predict there would be a plant person born that could specifically cause seeds to grow to maturity? Maureen had to have had those seeds for a long time, just waiting to use them again.

"Did you know what it was?" Devin continued his questioning.

"No. Not at all. I never knew it was a forbidden plant, and I sure didn't know that she was going to make it into poison," Mara quickly replied, begging Devin with her eyes to believe her. Mara was innocent. Devin didn't doubt that in the least.

"Where is this plant?" Devin asked.

"Over there, in the woods behind our house. Maureen didn't want it linked back to her, so she had us plant it here in the castoff camp. I later heard her tell someone that if the castoffs accidentally came upon it, that it would be a good thing to kill off as many of us as it could. That's when I knew what I had grown. We added extra thorny plants all around it to keep people away," Mara quickly added. "I don't want anyone near it. I hated when Colin would go and pick it for

Maureen. That plant scares me."

Devin nodded. He had been told how lethal it was, but Mara just confirmed what everyone had said. He didn't see it as her fault—she had done what she was told, and hadn't known any better—but would the elite see it that way? What she'd done was illegal, and she was already at the very edge of society as it was. What more could they do to punish her?

"How did Colin get roped into all of this?" Devin wondered. Colin was the assassin after all.

"After we grew the plant, and figured out what it was, we didn't know how to get rid of it. Colin agreed with me that it wasn't safe, so we went to Maureen and asked her to get rid of it," Mara explained. "I really had no clue how to kill it. We tried to dig it out, but it grew back. We stopped watering it, but only the plants around it died. We couldn't kill it."

"You thought you could ask her and she would do it?" Nessa asked. Maureen was good at playing nice, but even nice Maureen wasn't one you could ask such a thing of. She always had her reasons, and if she didn't suggest killing the plant, then she would have wanted it alive.

"Colin thought she had made a mistake. The plant was illegal to grow, or even possess. He was sure once we told her, she would be surprised and want to get rid of it," Mara replied caustically. "It wasn't a mistake. She wanted the plant, and by confronting her about it, we'd just made it worse. She told us that if we told anyone, she would claim that I stole the seeds and grew it on my own. She told me that her word, as the head of the elite, would be much more valuable than mine as a castoff. And she was right. As a castoff, we have no rights, and our word means nothing."

"But she was lying," Nessa replied, angry that the system could work that way. She'd never heard a castoff list a complaint before, but she had a hard time imagining that their word meant nothing.

A brief expression of disgust flashed across Mara's face, almost too fast to see. "But it was the truth. We left Maureen's home defeated, and placed as many thorny plants as we could around the poisonous one. We continued to hope that no one would ever find the plant, and everyone would stay safe. Unfortunately, that wasn't the case. Maureen returned to us and told us that for our insolence she would be requiring Colin to harvest the plant and place it in food at the palace."

"You knew it was poison by then," Nessa replied in shock. Mara had intentionally poisoned people if that was the case.

"And I told him not to. What more could she do to us?" Mara answered. She agreed completely with Nessa. "But Colin didn't see it that way. Maureen threatened us again with my family, and Colin being thrown out. Colin didn't want to poison anyone, but he did for our families."

Suddenly, Colin coughed behind Devin, and everyone turned to watch him gasp for air as he woke. Slowly, he sat up, shaking his head. Mara hurried over to sit beside him, placing her arm around his back and supporting him. He was weak, but awake and alive. She couldn't have hoped for anything more. Tears of happiness trickled down her cheeks.

"I didn't do it for my family," Colin said in a raspy voice. "I did it for Mara. Maureen told me that if I didn't act as the assassin, she would tell everyone Mara had grown an outlawed plant. The only punishment we have left as castoffs are our lives. If I didn't kill the elite, then Maureen would make sure that they killed Mara. I couldn't let her die. I can't live without her." Colin coughed a few more times, and finally caught his breath.

"Did Maureen tell you who to kill?" Devin asked.

"Yes. This was all planned. She never told me why, but I arrived early a few times to overhear her telling someone what she was doing," Colin replied.

"Do you know who?" Nessa asked. There could be hundreds of sidhe that Maureen would want to know. They had caught the assassin, but that still meant a traitor was out there.

"I never saw them. In fact, I don't know if the person was even around. It was like she was talking into the air, and when I entered, she would just turn to me and pretend she hadn't been talking to someone. I swear there was no one there. She was alone and just holding something in her hands. But I know there's no spell like that. I kind of thought she was just crazy." Colin described his odd encounters with Maureen. "She was like that a lot."

"What did you overhear?" Devin added to keep the conversation on track.

"That the plan was to kill off all of the younger sidhe," Colin replied. Surprised, Ness turned to Devin. It was just as he had suspected. How could he be so smart to pick up on that? "If there were no heirs left, each family would send a new ruling family to our village. Maureen seemed to be planning to take over, and she had the support of at least one village. The person she'd talked to was supposed to get more people or something along those lines. Unfortunately, I really didn't hear more than that. Right then, I knew who would be my targets before she even told me. There aren't many young left to each ruling family. I was relieved when you figured it out and took those last two children into your protection." Colin nodded to Devin. "Then there was no one left that she could order me to kill. I thought we were done, and that she had lost. But she didn't see it that way. She told me that I had to kill Fiona. I thought I'd heard her wrong ... hoped I'd heard her wrong. But I didn't. She really wanted Fiona dead. I'm happy she is not. Thank you, Day Human Prince, for saving her and the others, too. I may not like the elite, or agree with their rules, but that isn't a reason to murder. I didn't want to kill anyone. I didn't want any of them dead. Especially not you, Princess. However, I just couldn't let Maureen kill Mara."

Mara wrapped her arms tighter around Colin. Devin had all of his answers, and stood to walk out of the house. Nessa followed behind him, wondering what he was thinking now. She was tempted to peek into his mind, but knew it was easier to just ask.

'What's the plan?' she asked, sure that Devin had no intention of letting the two castoff sidhe die for what they'd done. Everything had been orchestrated by Maureen, all of the deaths were on her hands, yet Nessa didn't know what other choices there were.

'Is death really the only option?' Devin asked. He was planning something.

'For a castoff? Yes,' Nessa replied. *'We can't let them stay here, and the other villages wouldn't take them either. No matter if it's Maureen's fault or not, Mara grew an illegal plant and Colin killed people with its poison.'*

'And exile?' Devin asked. *'Is that an option?'*

'Exile is worse than death to the sidhe. This is our life, and there's nowhere that we fit in the day human world. The sidhe aren't made for your concrete cities. This is our home, and without a village to support them, it is death,' Nessa replied. Exile wasn't an option in Nessa's book.

Nodding, Devin turned back to the house, and saw that Mara was still on the floor with Colin.

"For now, you are both under house arrest," Devin told them, and they nodded their heads in reply. Instantly, Devin placed a barrier around the house. "You may receive food and drink through the spell, but you can't leave your house. Anyone can bring you food or water, but no one can enter.

Understand?"

"Yes," Colin replied, his voice less raspy.

"I'll have you brought before the council as soon as I can get them all together. We will get this done soon," Devin told them.

'What are you going to do?' Nessa asked.

'Be the king everyone expects me to be,' Devin replied.

CHAPTER 13

Nessa sat beside Devin in one of the two ornate seats on the stage of the amphitheater. It was slowly filling, and Devin was impatiently tapping his fingers beside her. Nessa took his hand to stop his fidgeting. She loved how rough it was; she could feel the years of hard work and training he had done. He had been trained for every type of situation, and was always perfect in how he handled it. How could he be nervous? He was much more of a man than anyone that entered, yet right now his confidence was not there, as she'd expected it to be. He smiled at her hand in his own, and her heart melted. Nessa loved Devin, even if she hadn't yet told him.

As Ronan entered with his father helping him, Devin stood and went to assist. Nessa remained seated, watching as Devin and Rolf settled Ronan in the front row. Her cousin was looking good considering that he had recently been on death's door ... even if he had a few less toes.

Nessa turned back to the people sitting around waiting. It was getting late for them. The sun was just beginning to rise. Most of them wanted to go back to bed, but none could deny Devin's request. Technically they could, but they feared him. Word had already gotten around that Maureen was dead, and that was enough to keep everyone there waiting for Devin to speak. Some had even started the rumor that he was responsible, but no one would directly say that to either Nessa or Devin. It wasn't a rumor, but she found it strange that most doubted Devin had to the power to do that, yet they all still feared him.

Devin quickly returned to Nessa's side, but he didn't sit. Instead, he looked around at the room of people, and nodded when Turner entered the back of the room with Colin and Mara. Nessa was surprised. Devin had said he would take care of them as soon as he could, but she'd expected him to address Maureen and the poisonings, not the punishment of the two castoffs. Devin briefly turned to Nessa, smiling to reassure her. His confidence was completely back.

"I'm thankful everyone could make it this late to meet. I called you all here to tell you that we no longer need to fear the assassin. The assassin, and those that hired him, have been caught and punished. The poison itself has been thrown out, and the plant that it was made from has been burnt to the ground," Devin began.

The sidhe faces stared at him. It was obvious none had been expecting things to be handled so quickly. Efficiency and effectiveness were not two traits of the sidhe. They were used to things drawing out for weeks or months, and many people dying in response. There needed to be retribution and payback before anyone would admit to any wrong doing, if anyone ever did. And to catch someone was even rarer. Doubt laced a few of the faces. It just wasn't their way.

"I have spoken with the assassin and gained insight as to how this was planned and how it all happened," Devin told the people. He motioned for Turner to bring the castoffs forward. Unafraid, Mara and Colin stood in front of the crowd. Nessa had no clue what the plan was, but it was obvious that Devin had shared it with them.

"Castoff Mara had been requested by her former family

leader, Maureen Ferguson, to grow an illegal plant. Mara's ability is to take seeds and grow them into plants. Maureen had hidden the seeds of the prohibited plant for years, and chose now to use them." Murmurs rose around the room. The sidhe never really liked direct facts, and since Maureen wasn't there to dispute it, none knew what to do. Devin ignored them and continued to talk. "Her husband, Colin, was recruited, at the threat of his wife being killed, to do the assassinations for the Ferguson family."

More talking erupted around them. Devin had just directly accused the Ferguson family of treason. Nessa tried to listen to the various conversations, and learned that they were all outraged that castoffs would accuse the dead Ferguson family leader of such a thing. To them it was blasphemy that the castoffs would even speak the dead lady's name. How could they attack the reputation of such a great lady that had recently passed on? Others were openly demanding that Colin and Mara be killed on the spot. They wanted justice for their dead. Devin didn't flinch at the talk, and waited patiently for the room to calm down. When he raised a hand, the room became silent again.

"I know exactly what you are all asking for, and sorry to disappoint you, but I have decided on a better punishment than death," Devin replied to those that had lost family in the scheme of Maureen's.

"How can anything be better than death for someone like them to say such lies?" Owen O'Ryan demanded. His voice and constant interruptions at any function was beginning to grate on Nessa's nerves. Owen was one of the only ones that still openly hated Devin. Nessa secretly wished he had been the one poisoned, or somehow implicated in the assassinations, and they could be rid of him.

"First off," Devin replied calmly; Owen didn't seem to

upset Devin as much as he upset Nessa, "they are not lies. While it was strenuous for her to get here, Fiona Ferguson is willing to testify that her mother planned everything." Fiona stood at the back of the room. Nessa hadn't even noticed her.

"My mother planned to kill off all of the remaining heirs to each family in order to allow outside families to start over here in the palace," Fiona said quietly. The room gasped in horror together. Not a single sidhe had come to that realization yet. "Including me." More people gasped. None could imagine killing off their own child.

"But …" Owen sputtered. He didn't have a quick comeback. That would have included him.

"You were the target, Owen," Fiona added. "You should be the one dead right now." That was enough to make the young O'Ryan sidhe sit back down. Suddenly, the cocky sidhe understood that it was his fault for his grandfather's death. The poisoned food had been meant for him.

"Back to the assassin and his wife," Devin continued, as if Owen had not interrupted him, "I have decided to exile them. They will be leaving immediately. I'll personally see that they are escorted far away from the sidhe so that we can continue our lives safely here."

Not a word was spoken around the room. It was quiet enough that you could hear a pin drop. The faces of the crowd stared at Devin in shock. Nessa even felt shaken. She had told Devin exile was worse than death. None had ever thought that a ruler would exile someone. The situation was more dire than they had expected. Soon the remaining Ferguson family members began to look around. They all remembered the promise that Devin had made to exile them for their leader's misdoings. Devin watched the Fergusons, and allowed them to worry for a few more minutes. Even Nessa was unsure if he would actually exile the entire family. Devin had asked her to trust him, and let him decide what needed to be done, but even she worried now. Fiona was carrying her dead brother's child, and part of Nessa didn't want Fiona thrown away to die alone. Nessa had never been really close with Fiona, but she was still family.

"As to the Ferguson family, Fiona has offered to go into exile to save the rest of you. She's willing to pay for her mother's crimes," Devin replied. Instantly, chaos broke out. It was too much for any of them to understand. He was going to throw out a pregnant woman.

Cries around them were of both fear and exuberance. The ones that thought they were exiled were now happy, but the others only saw that Devin was willing to toss out a pregnant woman on her own. That was a threat to everyone. If he was that hard and without feelings, then he truly meant everything he'd told them. He was a ruler to be feared.

'You can't do that to her,' Nessa complained silently from behind Devin.

'She asked to leave,' Devin responded waiting for the crowd to quiet.

'But you can't let her go off to die alone,' Nessa added. She really felt for Fiona.

'She isn't going to die. She's just getting a new life away from this. She'll be fine. I've made sure of it. All three of them will be safe, and will be allowed to start over. They will never be able to come back here, but they will be free and can live as they choose. Trust me,' Devin added, returning to Nessa's side and grabbing her hand.

Devin wasn't the heartless man everyone thought, but he wasn't about to correct the room. Nessa could already see that Devin was playing the role and using this as an opportunity to get the sidhe to understand and fear him even more.

"But what happens to the rest of us?" one of the Fergusons

asked from the front row. They didn't even seem to care what happened to Fiona, but only to themselves. That was the sidhe for you.

Nessa looked back up to Fiona in the last row. Was that why she wanted out? Did she understand what it was taking Nessa forever to grasp? The sidhe world was screwed up and needed to change. Fiona smiled at Nessa. She was happy with what Devin had said. Nessa felt that Devin was right. Fiona wanted out. *I'll be fine,* Fiona mouthed to Nessa.

Nessa had to smile. She would. How could there be anywhere in the world Fiona would not be fine? She was cunning and smart, and the day human world would just have to look out for her.

"The Ferguson village will be disbanded, and all will be required to move to a new village. In fact, I think none of the villages should be segregated based on family. It's time we change things around here, and Maureen gave us the best reason to do so. After the coronation, we will be implementing new rules, and a new way of do things. The sidhe are failing. You kill each other, and respond with retribution rather than justice. The sidhe world will evolve. It has to. For now, you may remain in your homes, but know that by next week it will change," Devin replied.

The faces of the elite palace sidhe just stared at him. They were not used to change, and definitely not used to things at such a fast pace. He was telling them the truth, yet many still couldn't grasp it. The older sidhe would never understand, but Devin didn't care. He looked around at the younger faces. The change would have to come by them. The sidhe world needed them, and there were six fewer left due to Maureen. They wouldn't let that happen again. The faces stared at the stage, waiting for Devin to say more. He did not. Helping Nessa to rise from her throne, he then led her out of the silent room.

"Are you serious?" Nessa whispered after they'd left.

"Absolutely," Devin replied. "Things need to change, and after the coronation we will change them. We will make this a night human world we can be proud of. We'll do it together." Devin bent down and kissed Nessa. She couldn't disagree with that.

Colin coughed, interrupting them. Devin pulled back from his kiss and smiled at Nessa.

"I'll be back in fifteen minutes. Just stay with Turner, and I'll come straight back to you when I return. I want to talk to you about something." Devin kissed her forehead quickly.

With that, he walked away with Colin, Mara, and Fiona behind him. Fiona stopped as they made their way out of view.

"Nessie, make sure to come visit us." Fiona rubbed her tummy and beamed at Nessa as they turned the corner and left.

"Where are they going?" Nessa asked Turner suspiciously. None of the three looked worried about starting over. How could that be? They wouldn't fit in too well in the day human world, no matter what Devin thought. They had no money, no career, no house or possessions—no way to survive.

"To my town, where else?" Turner asked like it wasn't a question. "My village is for all night and day humans who wish to live there. They'll be fine and fit in with everyone. My father is setting them up with a place to live and jobs to start off with. They now have the chance to make their own future outside of these walls." Turner offered Nessa his arm. Nessa accepted the gesture and let him walk her back to her room.

Devin returned from Triclan City, Turner's hometown, quicker than the fifteen minutes he'd expected it to take, and hoped that Turner had dropped Nessa off exactly where he'd asked. Getting Mara, Colin, and Fiona free of the sidhe was his first priority. Now, he needed to finally ask Nessa to marry him. The coronation was only a day away, and Devin wanted her to know that she was not alone. It wasn't that marriage was important, or urgent, since they were already bonded, but now was as good as any time to ask her. They could always wait—as he would always want her, and he always be bonded to her—but they didn't need to any longer. Devin loved Nessa, and he was sure she loved him, too. He didn't even bother to return to his room, but made his way out of the palace.

Ronan sat outside of the palace in the courtyard. He was enjoying the quiet of the day breaking and the sidhe all retiring to bed. He was in good spirits with the assassin caught and being allowed outside of Nessa's room.

"Are you finally going to ask her?" Ronan asked.

Devin grinned, and Ronan laughed.

"Just don't piss her off before you get the words out," Ronan teased as Devin ran out the gate and into the village.

For once, Devin didn't worry about that. It had been hours since their last fight. Something had changed, and they were getting along better. It was the right moment to ask.

Running through the village, Devin dodged the last few remaining sidhe. He couldn't wait to find Nessa and he didn't even look at the stray people he passed as he ran. The village was losing its awe and wonder, and was becoming home. He liked the common sidhe and couldn't wait to make changes to help them. Many bowed as he passed, and it was a little disappointing to find that they knew who he was now. He had hoped that wouldn't change things, but he had seen it with Colin. His title changed everything.

Devin made it to the bridge, and Turner came walking across it.

"She's alone?" Devin asked.

"I told Lindsey to scram as soon as you arrived. He just told me that you were here, so yes, all alone," Turner replied. "I guess this means you really are going to ask her?" Turner grinned.

Even Turner knew what the plan was. Turner, Gemma, and Ronan were all rooting for him. Devin was nervous, yet very excited. He was starting the change with the sidhe by changing his own life. Devin had never imagined being married, but now he couldn't imagine life without Nessa. Change was coming, and it was starting with him.

"Yes, I am," Devin replied, brushing his fingers through his dark blond hair. It was longer than he had ever had it as he'd had no time to get a haircut since he met Nessa, but she didn't mind. The sidhe wore their hair long enough to put into a ponytail, so even at the length it was, he still wasn't there yet. Devin took a deep breath and pushed Turner away.

Devin walked over the bridge that brought outsiders to the sidhe village. He could remember walking that bridge only days ago, not having the slightest clue that it would lead him to where he was now. He never thought he would be staying, let alone caring for the people beyond the bridge. More than that, he never thought Nessa would be his forever. Devin paused at the edge of the bridge. Nessa sat in the clearing, playing with the flowers that Mara had graciously put there for Devin. The field was a mixture of purple, pink, and blue. Her dark curls were a stark contrast to the light-colored flowers basking in the morning sun. Devin could have stood there and watched her for hours. He always saw her as a wood sprite when she was surrounded by nature. It was time to ask her. She didn't move as Devin approached.

"That was quick," Nessa replied when Devin stopped behind her. She didn't turn around but kept winding the flowers she picked into a crown.

"It didn't take much. They, all three, were really excited to be there. They basically pushed me out the door to start their new lives," Devin replied, moving in front of her. Nessa looked up at him and smiled. Returning the smile, Devin gently tugged on her curls, enjoying sitting amongst the flowers that now surrounded them.

"King Devin," Nessa teased as she placed the crown of flowers she was making on his head. "This is beautiful." She ran her hands over the flowers. They came in all shapes and sizes, and the sun rising on the horizon made Nessa's eyes sparkle as she looked at them. He didn't see the flowers any longer. All he saw was her.

Devin took her hands in his. The moment was perfect. He needed to tell her now.

"I never knew it was possible to love like this," Devin began. Nessa looked like she was going to speak, but Devin placed a finger on her lips. "I need to get this out." Nessa smiled and nodded. "You know about my past. You know that I was raised well and taken care of, but I never felt this emotion before. This is all new to me. I cared for Arianna, but there was nothing of the spark I feel with you. It's different when I touch your hand, or your face."

Devin gently rubbed his thumb along her cheek. Just that was enough to make him want to kiss her and forget everything he had planned. Nessa leaned into his hand. She enjoyed the feel of him as much as he enjoyed touching her. He had to stop or he would never get his question out.

"You have made me feel something I didn't know was possible. You make me into the man I want to be. You believe in me, you trust me, and you make me feel like I'm perfect for this world I know nothing about. Nessa, I didn't know I was lost before you came into my life, but let me tell you, I was. You found me."

Nessa smiled and took his hands in her own. She didn't interrupt him, but sat and listened. He could see her happiness at his words. The bond between them was open, and there was nothing hidden between them. He was speaking the truth and she knew it.

"I didn't know the first time I met you what it was I felt. The emotions that went through me were foreign. But I can tell you now. I love you. Vanessa McKinny, I love you."

Nessa leaned forward without replying and kissed Devin. His hands snaked to her waist and pulled her down on top of himself, onto the ground amongst the flowers they already crushed when they sat. His emotions were running wild, but so were hers. They were feeding off each other, and growing stronger together. Again he found himself completely distracted. Devin wanted to keep kissing her longer, but he was on a mission. He needed to ask her. Devin sat them both back up and pulled back just a little. The contact made him want to continue kissing her, but he needed her to know exactly how much he loved her.

"What?" she asked, wondering why he'd suddenly stopped.

"I need to finish what I came here to say. You are such a distraction," Devin replied. Nessa grinned and sat back on the grass across from him. She found his need to talk amusing. Devin couldn't help but grin back. "I love you, and need you in my life. This bond between us is forever, and I know you'll always be mine. But I want more."

Nessa's eyes grew big. She finally understood how serious he was. The moment they both had been waiting for was there. Devin could ask her, and she was willing to accept his proposal.

"Aye." A male voice called from across the glen. "Is that you, little Nessie?"

Nessa's concentration on Devin shifted to the new arrival. Devin turned to see who it was. Personally, he wanted to hit any person that was dense enough to interrupt them. Two lovers rolling in the grass was not something you interrupted.

"Sorry," Nessa whispered as she stood and greeted the man who approached. He was big and burly with curly red hair on his head and face. As he got closer, Devin noticed he had to only be in his twenties, but was built like an ox.

"Liam?" Nessa guessed, finally recognizing the man. The man wasn't from their village, yet Nessa knew him.

Grinning, he stooped down to hug her. He picked her right off the ground and twirled her in a circle. He was too comfortable with Nessa for Devin's taste. Devin stood and clenched his fists. His perfect moment was being ruined by a big ox that insisted on touching his girl.

'He's from one of the other villages,' Nessa told Devin silently. *'He's a family friend, and just that.'* Nessa had to have felt Devin's jealously.

"I knew you wouldn't forget me. My pa told me that I shouldn't expect much since it's been over ten years, and you were but a wee girl at the time, but I was sure that you'd remember me. I'm not the forgettable type," Liam told her. He was quite full of himself.

Nessa blushed as she was sat back on the ground from his big, long-lasting hug. Liam didn't even attempt to introduce himself to Devin. He wanted to cough to get their attention, but in reality he just wanted the big oaf to move along. Devin was close to asking Nessa to marry him. The timing was right, and he was sure she was going to say yes. Devin stood and waited as Liam continued to talk. Couldn't the big ox just move along?

"How could I forget you?" Nessa asked. That stung a bit for Devin. "You were the only one who actually stood up to Rhys when I was younger." Devin's jealously softened a bit. He knew how harsh Rhys could be with her when she was young. Anyone that helped her, she would remember.

"Well, he needed a little beat down after he was being rude.

No lady should be treated that way," Liam laughed. He obviously had not forgotten the incident either.

"I wouldn't have classified myself as a lady," Nessa replied with her own laugh. Devin tried to wait patiently for the red-haired fellow to leave. "What are you doing here?" Nessa finally asked what Devin wanted to know. The sidhe didn't commonly visit the other villages.

"Coming to your coronation, of course. I wouldn't miss it for the world. Only wish Rhys was around to see it, too. Can you imagine how upset he would be right now?" Liam laughed a deep, hearty laugh. Nessa joined in the laughter, but Devin did not. He was early, and Devin didn't appreciate that. It made it seem like this oaf of a man had some hidden intention. Devin hated the sidhe and their hidden agendas.

"Then your father isn't coming?" Nessa asked, seeming a little disappointed. Devin appreciated that she wanted to see the father more than the ox.

"No, I insisted I be able to represent the family," Liam replied. Nessa nodded with a smile. Obviously, they were old friends. "Because I could only do this in person." Liam bowed down to Nessa. "I ask formally, Vanessa McKinny, since you are unwed, may I court you?"

Coming in 2015:
The Day Human Way
(Book 3 of The Day Human Trilogy)

ACKNOWLEDGEMENTS

To you, the reader. Thank you for taking the time to read this story and go on the journey with me. If you liked it, please leave a review on your favorite online bookseller (or all of them!) and connect with me social media. The greatest help you can do to keep a writer going is to support them by spreading the word about their books and leaving them encouraging words.

Also I would like to thank my editors and cover designers. A good editor is essential to getting the story correct (and in my case- two editors). Thank you so much, Kathie at Kat's Eye Editing and Melissa at There for You Editing. They made the book just that much stronger and such a better story that you all got to read. It would not be the same book without them. Also a thanks to my proofer Ashton Brammer for going over the novel with a fine tooth comb to catch little errors that bug people. A thank-you to my *AMAZING* cover artist Ravven for such a pretty cover. She puts so much detail into every cover-I can't say how lucky I am to work with her! A great cover helps get people interested. They may say *never judge a book by its cover*, but everyone does! I greatly appreciate all those that can do what I cannot, like editors and cover designers. I'm grateful I was able to find great professionals to work with on this book.

I'd also like to thank my hubby for continuing to push me further down the writing road. He gives me time when I need it to work on my stories. He encourages me to keep going each and every day on this adventure. And he does all the behind-the-scenes effort to make this work (have you seen my trailers- he is awesome!). This would be so much harder without his help. So thank you, B. for pushing me off the deep end (or the cliff as I see it sometimes). And a great big thanks to my little munchkins who keep me going from before the sun comes up 'til long after it sets. Love you AK and KB.

Thank you so much for taking the time to read my novel!!

ABOUT B KRISTIN McMICHAEL

Originally from Wisconsin, B. Kristin currently resides in Ohio with her husband, two small children, and three cats. When not doing the mom thing of chasing kids, baking cookies, and playing outside, she is using her PhD in biology as a scientist.

In her free time she is currently hard at work on multiple novels. Every day is a new writing adventure. She is a fan of all YA/NA fantasy and science fiction and continues to promote good indie books on her own blog at www.bkristinmcmichael.com. You can find her on Twitter, Facebook, and Goodreads.

Other books by this author:
- To Stand Beside Her
- The Blue Eyes Trilogy
  - The Legend of the Blue Eyes
  - Becoming a Legend
  - Winning the Legend
- The Day Human Trilogy
  - The Day Human Prince
  - The Day Human King
  - The Day Human Way (2015)
- The Chalcedony Chronicles
  - Carnelian
  - Chrysoprase
  - Aventurine (2015)
  - Unnamed (2015)